Discover for yourself why readers can't get enough of the multiple award-winning publisher Ellora's Cave. Whether you prefer e-books or paperbacks, be sure to visit EC on the web at www.ellorascave.com for an erotic reading experience that will leave you breathless.

www.ellorascave.com

D0733850

STEPHANIE'S MENAGE
An Ellora's Cave Publication, August 2004

Ellora's Cave Publishing, Inc.
1337 Commerce Drive, Suite 13
Stow, OH 44224

ISBN #1-4199-5013-4

ISBN MS Reader (LIT) ISBN # 1-84360-315-2
Mobipocket (PRC) ISBN # 1-84360-316-0

Other available formats (no ISBNs are assigned):
Adobe (PDF), Rocketbook (RB), Mobipocket (PRC) & HTML

STEPHANIE'S MENAGE © 2003, MARI BYRNE

ALL RIGHTS RESERVED. This book may not be reproduced in whole or in part without permission.

This book is a work of fiction and any resemblance to persons, living or dead, or places, events or locales is purely coincidental. They are productions of the authors' imagination and used fictitiously.

Edited by *Marty Klopfenstein*
Cover art by *Darrell King*

Warning:

The following material contains graphic sexual content meant for mature readers. *Stephanie's Ménage* has been rated E-rotic by a minimum of three independent reviewers.

Ellora's Cave Publishing offers three levels of Romantica™ reading entertainment: S (S-ensuous), E (E-rotic), and X (X-treme).

S-*ensuous* love scenes are explicit and leave nothing to the imagination.

E-*rotic* love scenes are explicit, leave nothing to the imagination, and are high in volume per the overall word count. In addition, some E-rated titles might contain fantasy material that some readers find objectionable, such as bondage, submission, same sex encounters, forced seductions, etc. E-rated titles are the most graphic titles we carry; it is common, for instance, for an author to use words such as "fucking", "cock", "pussy", etc., within their work of literature.

X-*treme* titles differ from E-rated titles only in plot premise and storyline execution. Unlike E-rated titles, stories designated with the letter X tend to contain controversial subject matter not for the faint of heart.

STEPHANIE'S MÉNAGE

Mari Byrne

Dedication

To: T, C, & T, Angela's SPs, Ms. Roberts, Ms. Smith, and DezDot
Many thanks for encouraging my dream!

Special thanks to Liddy, Boot Camp instructor Extraordinaire.

Treva, who always answers my cries.

And Ann, who should win a medal for this one!

Prologue

"You shame our people by suggesting there is not one single woman in our entire world good enough to be your bride." The Queen's flowing gown twirled as she turned sharply in her pacing. "Why must you go to the mortal world? There are plenty here in Aranak who would give their daughters to you both."

"Mother. We've had this conversation before," Kristain started out calmly. "This family, this Monarchy, needs new blood." He paused and gave her a disgusted look. "Hell, for that matter, this World needs new blood and well you know it. You must see this is the only way."

Without looking away from his mother, Kristain, using the telepathic link every twin on Aranak is born with, asked Mitch to stand beside him.

Mitch lazily straightened from his lounging position and strolled leisurely over to stand at his brother's side.

I don't care if she can hear us or not. Kristain stated, his calmness disintegrating. *We're going, and in this she has no say.*

Brother mine, Mitch answered sarcastically, *you preach to the converted. You need to tell your Queen, not me.*

For reasons beyond Kristain's understanding, their mother couldn't always read her people, let alone her own children, though the reading of all her peoples' minds should have come with her acceptance of the crown.

Mitch watched as his mother came to an abrupt stop, then with a quiet menace about her, turned around looking from one son to the other.

"You have already made your choice and nothing I say will change your mind."

The two brothers stared back impassively.

"So be it. The consequences are yours to bear." With those last words she went to a door, hidden behind her throne and stormed through it, slamming it behind her.

Kristain stared after their retreating mother for a moment, then turned to Mitch.

"Well, that went well. Shall we go then?"

Mitch slapped his brother on the back and turned him toward the door. "And here I thought you were going to be the one to convince her. But now I see the only way we'll ever convince *Queen Sara* of our determination to seek a bride elsewhere is when we present our bride as a *fait accompli*."

Kristain sighed heavily, "I thought perhaps she would be more amenable to the idea if we gave her time." He started toward the door. "Now I see our trip through the portal is the only way she'll take us seriously."

Mitch nodded his head in agreement. "We have to start somewhere and I've always had a good feeling about Earth. We'll find our mate there. I know it."

So, this is Earth? Mitch looked around as he and Kristain made their way toward the buildings ahead of them in the distance.

It wasn't so very different from Aranak.

Kristain turned and Mitch heard his thoughts. *In fact, I think there might be even less difference than we previously thought. I don't think it'll take very long for us to find our bride and return home.*

Mitch turned his gaze away from an intriguing woman who had caught his eye as he scoped the lay of the land and eyed his brother skeptically. *Let us hope so. I don't want to spend more time away from home than we have to. The laws Mother could implement while we're gone stagger my imagination.*

Kristain nodded in agreement. Both men squared their shoulders, and readied themselves for the search to come.

* * * * *

"Defy me, will they! They think I'm so out of touch with my people I don't know what is said? Damn ungrateful *frechie* twins! Those two have absolutely no respect for their mother!" Sara strode in half circles around the luxuriously appointed suite of rooms, taking things at will and dashing them against the farthest wall she could reach.

"My own flesh and blood defies me at every turn!" Sara shrieked. "Their father Dain was the same. I don't care how the people suffer! They were put here for ME! They serve MY pleasure!" Picking up a priceless object, Sara cocked her arm back and threw it at the door as hard as she could. Mere seconds after the crash, the door opened.

"Temper, temper, QUEEN Sara," a thin voice chided. "Where is the stunning beauty with grace, poise, and infinite patience, the one I crowned so long ago?" The new arrival shuffled her way toward Sara, who once again was reaching out for the nearest object. Her choice was indeed poor, for she picked up a thin glass bell, one in danger of shattering at the slightest touch.

"Don't even think it!" The brittle voice shrieked.

Sara froze in her tracks as the voice, laced with fury, bellowed the warning.

Turning her head slowly, Sara looked toward the old crone whose voice had moments ago been that of an old and frail woman and suddenly was that of a vengeful mother hellbent on murder.

Shakily, Sara looked toward her hand where she held the "Bell of Coronation". In her rage she had picked up the one object guaranteed to bring about the fall of her own empire. The legend of the bell held that if the bell peals when a new queen rings it at her inauguration, she is the true queen. If, however, a queen who is not the true queen rings the bell, the jewel will shatter.

"Why?" Sara growled, and cupping the object to study it, seemed to wilt.

The paper-thin beveled glass she held was a thing of Beauty. Rimmed with 24kt. solid gold and crowned at the top of the handle with four stones. An emerald, a ruby, and a diamond, with a fourth stone atop the three as the *pièce de résistance*. The fourth stone, called a *zarak*, named for its creation close to the mountains of Zarnak, came from the farthest regions of Azaya. Very few of the gemstones existed. *Zarak* took on the color of its surroundings and shimmered more brilliantly than a diamond. There were only two like it in The Royal Aranak collection. One, the largest *zarak* ever found, could be found in the scepter, while the second stone topped the Bell of Coronation.

"I mean, it's gorgeous and all, but it only ever rang once for me." Years of frustrated pain laced her voice.

The Crone spoke once again, still without sympathy in her voice.

"I told you. In our bargain, you knew that it would only ever ring once. You agreed that it was all you wanted. Besides, it is part of the royal collection and would be sorely missed were it to break. Do not blame me now if you aren't satisfied with the bargain."

Anger sounded in Sara's voice as she spoke now.

"Do not preach to me. I want it to ring again. I want it to sound out through the halls of this palace and the countryside and let the people of Aranak know that *I* am the true queen. No one can take my place." Since the inauguration, any time the queen had touched it, no sound emitted from the priceless artifact.

"You agreed to the terms and you know you can't go back on them. It is done and no amount of screaming and raging at your fate will change that." The Crone paused. "Move on and use that rage to further your desires."

To the Crone, the magic that had allowed Sara to get what she wanted was the bottom line. The deal they had struck had given Sara what she wanted, and the Crone the leftovers. Sara thought it was a perfect bargain and the Crone was more than happy for Sara to think her motives, or the payoff, were nothing for the Crone.

The old woman watched as Sara, resigned now, slowly replaced the priceless artifact in its pillowed niche.

"Now," the voice of the crone was once again thin and wavery. "If you've had enough acting like a two year old spoiled brat, I do believe there was something you wanted to discuss." The old hag resumed her shuffling walk as she spoke and now stopped at a chair resplendent in silk and satin fabrics. The poor, starved and downtrodden laborers who had slaved over the fabric were merely the tiniest faction of the realm this Queen had angered, ostracized, or outright beat into submission.

"Tell me Sara, would this display have anything to do with your sons being unenlightened in regards to what extent you've driven the Queendom of Aranak and its people? The fighting between Aranak and the Horrdian people over a slight done to your ego? The revenue generated by laws created to stock your coffers instead of our Queendom?" A sly smile played across the old woman's wrinkled lips, "Or perhaps your penchant to pick only from the line of the royal families for your playthings? Systematic slaughter in anything is a true form of art in my mind, but would it be to your sons?"

"Damn you. No. They know nothing but what I want them to know. This has only to do with them choosing my successor. It's enough I have to deal with those two, now they want me to give up all I hold dear! It's enough to drive a mother to homicide."

"There, there, dear. Let us speak of other things." The old crone soothed the woman who would see the downfall of not only her children, but also the Empire this unfit Queen had begun to destroy some twenty years ago.

It didn't take much to distract Sara from her anger as the Crone had learned over the years. This time, she had ammunition that would drive Queen Sara wild.

"If there's nothing else you'd care to discuss, I have a little treat for you. A little something which came into my care that I'd like to leave with you. Since we'll eventually need someone to give its life for our little plan to work, I thought you'd like to get what you could out of it first."

"A treat? For me? I thought you were just going to use one of the Horrd peasants for the ritual. It shouldn't take more than a lowly servant to propel you to the Earth realm in order to interfere with Mitch and Kristain."

"Well dear, this subject should do nicely. He has a touch of royal blood and a body…well, look for yourself." With a wave of her gnarled fist, the Crone opened a door and Sara watched in glee as a virile young man walked through it.

Ahhh…Dorian Goreon. A distant cousin of her husbands and with a body she had kept a lecherous eye on for some time now. A fine, sculpted specimen of a young man, one who would serve both their purposes well.

"Come forward, young man." Sara barely noticed the excited thrill in her voice and congratulated herself. Her voice sounded as strong and youthful as it had twenty years ago when she'd made the deal with the old Crone to kill her remaining husband and rule alone.

Thank the gods Laric, her husband's twin, had died early and she hadn't needed to go through with the planned double marriage. The brothers might have been her mates, if not exactly *her* chosen mates. Besides, she hadn't cared for the fact she would have two men hounding her after they were married. No, the two were stepping-stones to the throne and she had gone along with the marriage plans for that reason alone.

After she and Dain had married, and once she'd had her twins, it had been all she could do not to crow at the fact Laric had died early. She didn't know what all the fuss had been about over finding your chosen ones, even if her mates had seemed happy enough. She hadn't felt much of anything except joy at finally finding a means to gaining her throne.

Her only regret was she hadn't had girls before Laric or Dain's death. Her lineage wouldn't truly be carried on through her own offspring. No, the "fresh blood" her Horrd-like son Mitch and his prissy brother Kristain were insisting on would bastardize her lineage instead.

A smile grew wide on her face and she began to giggle at thoughts of the ritual she would soon undertake to thwart her sons' plan.

"Yes, Lovely." Sara said as her full attention returned to the young man. She enjoyed giving them a secret nickname before the playtime began. She would appreciate this one fully before his time came to die.

"Yes, My Queen. What will you have of me?"

His deep voice sent shivers of pleasure straight to her already wet pussy. So caught up in the feast laid out before her, she reached down to touch herself. She continued to build the tension strumming between her legs with her own hand as she spoke.

"Strip and stretch yourself fully!" Still stroking herself in pleasure, she reached out to grasp the short bullwhip sitting on a table beside her. The sound of the leather snapping on flesh was one of the most sinful sounds she had ever heard. And soon, it would be the sound of the lash hitting her toy's flesh that brought her to her ultimate satisfaction.

Sara's eyes glazed slightly as she watched the man before her disrobe thoroughly and take his hard length in his hand while beginning to massage it. No thought was given to the old woman who even now watched with jaded eyes. No, Sara's only thoughts were for the cock now stretching before her hungry stare.

He would understand before long what would happen if he came too quickly. Sara would enjoy stripping his skin from his body. But it wouldn't matter one way or the other what the man did. The young stud before her would soon be dying a bloody death.

The Crone chanted verses in an ancient tongue as Sara rode the young stallion's phallus for the seventeenth time that night. The young man had indeed been virile for he had refused every drop of the aphrodisiac offered.

Not that it mattered anyway. All that had been in the tonic was something to make his shaft hard for a long period of time. The Crone knew it was the degrading sexual acts themselves that built the power. Anything to make the participants uncomfortable, even their arousal, fed the ritual as nothing else could.

It was a blessing the Queen favored her pleasures on the rougher side and it wasn't long before the Crone's ears perked up as she heard the all too familiar pant and moan of climax.

Reaching into the folds of her *franki*, the ritual robe of an Aranak Witchling, for the *harkie* dagger, she waited patiently, kneeling at the head of the youth. The ritual words and the *harkie* would send the soul of Sara's stud to the realm the brothers had passed into and allow the Crone to guide him to do her bidding.

Thinking only of the ritual soon to be performed, the Crone slowly brought the dagger over Lovely's head continuing the chant, and waited for the scream of his climax. Soon, she too would have all she desired.

Sara threw her head back as her hips ground down on Lovely's large cock seeking her ultimate pleasure. Climax!

Hearing a hard gasping moan escape from the man under her, she dropped her head forward with the intention of admonishing her stallion not to erupt before she did, only to stare into the gleaming edge of a blade.

The Crone knelt at the head of Lovely waiting for just the right moment to slit his throat. Anger churned inside her, almost completely obliterating her feelings of sweet agony. Her first thought was to reach out and grab the dagger from the Crone and toss it to the side where she had no way of interfering in Sara's fun. Instead, she glared hard at her and shouted.

"Let it be!" Sara's hips continued to rock back and forth as she spat her orders out at the Crone. "Leave us! NOW! When I have finished, you may then proceed! Not a moment before…aaahhhh!"

Sara's voice raised an octave as Lovely ground his pelvis upward, slamming his cock harder into her cunt. Her only thought when she caught her breath was if Lovely wanted it rough, she'd sure as hell accommodate him!

Panting as she spoke, Sara reached for her own weapon as she watched the Crone scuttle back in horror at the look she saw on Sara's face.

"That's right bitch! Baaaaack offff!" Her orgasm was right on top of her and so close to breaking the tiniest movement would set her off. She tried to still the youth beneath her with pressure from her thighs, but he was having none of it. He pumped his hips faster and harder causing Sara to reach down to grasp onto his shoulders in an effort to hang on.

He too was close to climax and wouldn't be denied. Thrusting harshly, breath coming in great big gasps, it took two more pumps of his hips to have them both screaming out their releases in long, painful, wheezes.

When some semblance of normal breathing returned and the blackness receded from her vision, Sara looked down at Lovely lying underneath her and spoke.

"It's a shame you just did that." She purred softly. "While wonderful, I told you not to come before I had given permission. For this infraction, you'll receive the end of my lash once again, and we'll start at the beginning. We'll go all night until you get it right if we have to."

The young man looked up at her, swallowing to ease the dryness in his mouth. When he finally spoke, his voice croaked.

"Yes, your Majesty. Punish me if you must."

It was the answer Sara wanted to hear. It really was too bad he would be dead come morning.

Sara looked to the Crone who now crouched in the corner a bit further from Lovely and herself, and smiled.

"If you'll wait, you won't be disappointed. Have patience."

The Crone nodded and watched as once again the two bodies began their dance. Again.

The body lay still as Sara gazed down in fascination. This wasn't the first time she had seen a dead body and she knew it wouldn't be the last. It continuously amazed her that she could kill so easily and feel nothing. After Dain's death, she had vowed to do anything to hold the throne, and she would, even if it meant the death of a worthy co-conspirator.

The Crone had given her an excuse for the many untold hours of pleasure she'd received from the young men and women she'd consumed—as well as providing her with delightfully creative ways to torture peasants and titled subjects alike.

It was a shame but… Shrugging indifferently, Sara clapped her hands loudly and the door opened immediately.

"Take that—" she waved a hand in the direction of the body of the old Crone while she walked toward a door, "…out. And have someone clean up this mess immediately."

Opening the door now in front of her, she entered an attached room and shut the door behind her. Looking toward a rack on the far wall, the main focus of the room, she smiled at the young men hanging from shackles.

The privilege of her crown was indeed such a pleasure. Smiling, she inspected her choices, as well as her favorite implements of torture in a room full of them. The metal rods of discipline she preferred sizzled nicely in red-hot coals kept that way by servants she never saw.

"Now that the sacrifice is complete, and my plans set into motion, I'm ready for some more sport. Which tasty morsel shall

I sample from this rousing set of 'Cock and Balls'?" Sara chuckled as she walked toward the naked bodies hanging on the wall.

"Which of you treats shall tempt my eager palate tonight? Hmmm?" Her hand stroked over a bulging male pec, tweaking the clamp attached to a nipple. She trailed her finger through blood dripping from a pierced ring downward making a trail along the chest and stopping just above a jutting cock.

"I'm pleased you are so eager to see me again. You can provide me with more pleasure than the Crone ever did. Show me you were worth her sacrifice."

Wrapping her hand around the man's pride, she gave his dick a few strokes with one hand and fingered his balls with the other.

"I must admit I am delighted you're finally up for another round. I could go all night and happily go through the day tomorrow! None of you have yet to bore me, and I'm so very glad I've kept you all around for a bit longer tonight." Her tone was matter of fact while still carrying a malicious undertone of sexual tension.

Sighing heavily, Sara let go of her toy and turning her head from side to side, assessed her choices. Shrugging, Sara chose the rod closest to her heating up in the burning coals. Turning her head briefly, she watched as the end glowed bright red and a thin trail of smoke rose up from the branding rod she pulled from the heat. Smiling winningly, she brought the fired rod up to the flesh in front of her while stroking the penis in her other hand harder, bringing a moan of painful pleasure from her victim.

"Now that the preliminaries are over, are you ready for the real fun to begin?"

The screams the inhabitants of the castle listened to coming from the Queen's chambers were ignored, just as they had been every other time they were heard. Those who had lengthy memories crossed themselves and thanked their gods it wasn't them offering up delights to the Queen as they scurried to attend to their own duties.

* * * * *

Sometime later, the bloodied figure collapsed against the wall in exhaustion. Blood streamed from him, even as pain throbbed in places he hadn't even known could be hurt. He had to get to Shan Lin and Vincent. Those twins were of the very few who could get a message to the Princes about the Queen and her plans.

Slowing his labored breathing as best he could, the man used the last of his strength to push himself away from the wall and stumbled onward. The Twin Warriors might be the Princes' last hope.

Vincent woke at the uneven tapping on the door. The shack they had been given by the Queen's aide for quarters wouldn't have housed a goat comfortably, and any sound made was quickly amplified into a thunderous cacophony.

It was true both he and his brother had become used to more comfortable surroundings; but, it hadn't taken them very long to settle back into the routine of living in inhospitable places.

Unwrapping himself from the thin fur he'd brought with him, Vincent got up, picked up his sword and on silent feet went to a slit in the wall to find out who, or what, had disturbed them.

Propped against the door, the shape of a man could barely be discerned under the crust of dried blood coating a slumping body.

Shan Lin! Wake! Vincent called to his brother through their link.

From the corner of his eye, Vincent watched as Shan Lin moved immediately to a defensive crouch.

What is it brother? More Horrd come for a rematch?

Vincent gave a silent laugh as he answered.

No, Shan Lin. If anything, they've sent us one of their victims as an ambush.

The uneven tapping continued, as if whoever stood at the door was desperate for someone to be there. Shan Lin went on silent feet to stand near the other side of the door.

Ready whenever you are. Vincent heard his brother's soft words in his mind. Vincent reached his hand out to the latch even as he continued to watch through the slit. As quick as he could, he jerked on the latch and the door slammed open into the room's wall. A body fell through the opening onto the floor and emitted a torturous groan of pain.

He knelt by the body and felt Shan Lin brush by him, on his way out the door. He knew his brother would locate any enemies lurking in the shadows.

Vincent ran his hands lightly over the figure on the floor, checking for traps. All he could find was blood and bits of flesh clinging to the person lying before him.

Vincent started to stand, wiping the gore on his own clothing, when he heard a whisper.

"What?" He bent closer, ready in case the blood, which covered the body, didn't belong to the person lying on the floor.

"Try again. I can barely hear you." Bending closer, he cocked his ear toward the figure in an attempt to hear better.

"Vin…Queen…kill Mit…Kri…get warriorsssss…" The words trailed off into a hiss, then stopped altogether as the man sank into unconsciousness.

Vincent looked down at the mess in front of him, a recognition coming into his eyes, and swore softly.

Shan Lin came back in just as Vincent picked the body up gently and placed it on a scarred table at the far side of the room.

"What's up with…that?" Shan Lin gestured to the figure Vincent draped on the table.

"Help me clean him up. I think I know who it is, and whatever he was babbling about has to do with the Queen, Mitch, Kristain, and death." Even as he spoke, Vincent ran over to their supplies to dig for their emergency kit.

"And if it's what I think has happened, we're going to need all the information he can give us."

Chapter 1

"Now that we're here, we need to fit in. Clothes, a place to stay, transportation, and learning a little Earth lingo would help. The woman we're searching for needs to know we can blend in to any surrounding. We want to be an asset to our Queen."

Kristain nodded as they surveyed their surroundings.

"I agree. Let's see if we can't find out what currency they deal in."

Walking forward, the brothers went to make a life for themselves in the Earth's realm and find their bride.

It took them longer than they had anticipated to establish themselves as two rich businessmen with nothing better to do with their time than play. Once they were settled, their search for a bride had begun in a surprising direction.

Babbet Carlson turned out to be the antithesis of what they agreed was their perfect mate. She was conniving, manipulative, and cruel. Her taste in sexual conduct was selfish, perverse, and often sadistic.

Both Mitch and Kristain had a taste for bondage, but not to the extent Babbet enjoyed it. Their first taste of Babbet's proclivities had been a surprise. The second called an end to their liaison.

The three had been having a raunchy bout of sex which seemed to satisfy the craving both men had begun to notice in Babbet when, from some hidden place in her bed, she pulled out a short stake and begun to drag it across Kristain's haunches.

"*Riad*! What the hell?" Kristain slapped a hand against his ass as pain shot up through his buttocks. Bringing his hand up to inspect it, he found the wet stickiness of blood blooming on his hand.

The look of puzzled pain that Kristain gave Babbet intensified as he found the sharp stake still in her grip.

"Either your nails need cutting, or *that* doesn't belong in this bed!"

Setting down the stake, Babbet took one look at the blood on Kristain's hand, moved her hips against Kristain's rapidly retreating cock. Bringing his hand to her mouth, she licked at the blood.

"Hey! Stop it, woman! What the...unggggh." Kristain tried to jerk his hand from Babbet but was unable to stop her frenzied movements.

It didn't take long before she cried out her release, and cooed her praise to Kristain.

"Oooo. That was amazing. I don't think I've ever had a harder release. A little blood in the mix is always..." Her words trailed off as he pushed off the bed and strode angrily toward her bathroom.

Mitch, who had been waiting to join in with Babbet and Kristain, picked up the stake she'd laid aside, and began to get an idea of just what the woman was into. It wasn't necessarily he and his brother weren't into kink, because they were. It just wasn't the same kink Babbet was into. They didn't feel the need to inflict pain the way she appeared to, and it explained the uncertain feelings they initially had about her.

Damn if this woman didn't parallel their mother a little too much for Mitch's tastes. Then again, perhaps it was only one incident. A woman in the heat of passion could be excused the first time for over enthusiasm. If not, best to find out now.

Babbet paced the hallway as she waited for Kristain and Mitch to come down the stairway of her home. She tried to guess every reason the two men could come up with for leaving, and continually went back to the Bone Scratcher she had used on Kristain two nights before.

She had assumed both men were into a little more kink than they were, and her assumption had apparently been very costly.

She now wondered if she shouldn't have asked, or even eased them into the kind of bed games she enjoyed, no—craved. But Babbet had always gotten her way in the bedroom before, by dominance or torture, whichever worked on the individual man she was with.

Even after both men had returned from the bathroom that night, and Kristain had bowed out, Mitch had explained neither man was into actual pain with their pleasure. If it was a problem for Babbet, she needed to speak up now, and they would end their affair so she could find a man or men to indulge herself in her desires.

Even as Mitch spoke, Babbet had shaken her head and gone to stop Kristain from leaving.

"Really, Kristain. It was only a little bit of blood. It enhances the sex and I like the taste. You could try just a…"

"Woman, are you out of your mind? I should have made it clear from the beginning. No blood. But by *Riad*, I won't let you gouge me again!"

"Please. I won't. Mitch?" Babbet turned to the second twin. "Talk to him. Tell him I mean it. I'll make it up to you both." Tears formed in her eyes, falling in rivulets down her cheek.

The men each looked to the other, and then at Babbet, whose tears continued to stream down her cheeks just as she'd planned, and sought to soothe away her supposed genuine concern.

Babbet had smiled through her tears.

"Anything you want. I'll let you do with me as you both please."

"Well now. If you're serious Babbet, there are better ways to feel pain that don't actually hurt."

Mitch walked up to Babbet and grasped both her hands in one of his.

"Well, not much anyway. But you'll still get the same pleasure from the pain we'll inflict."

Kristain smiled toward his brother, then walked over to join the pair.

"And I'll be more than happy to show you the error of your ways."

Kristain swung his arm back and brought it down across Babbet's ass with a satisfying smack.

Babbet shivered as she felt the stinging pain travel through her bottom toward her quivering thighs.

In a voice rough with lust she purred her pleasure to the pair.

"Thank you, Master. More please."

Now she wondered if she shouldn't have just gone on with their vanilla kinks for a short time as opposed to her darker ones she had injected again in a frenzy of lust.

She turned to the stairway when she heard the first footstep on the top step and rushed to cling to the balustrade, which stood sentinel at the bottom of the stairway. She looked up to find Mitch behind Kristain, both men carrying the luggage they had come with.

Kristain started down the stairway to see Babbet was having difficulty keeping the temper out of her eyes and voice. She looked prepared to beg the two men to stay, and the idea seemed to leave a bad taste in her mouth. To Kristain, it clearly showed on her face.

"Please!" She began as Mitch stepped behind Kristain and began his descent. "Whatever you ask, whatever you want, I'll do it. Just please stay. You two are the only men in my entire sexual experience to give me an orgasm, to bring out the woman in me. I am begging you to reconsider." Her tears fell, and the pain of the two men leaving leaked through her voice.

Kristain stopped two steps from the bottom and Mitch a few behind him. He looked at the woman who had bloodied him and his brother one time too many, and turned the look of an angry prince on her rather than that of a lover.

"Madame. You were asked, and warned, my brother and I were not to be bloodied. Instead of adhering to our wishes, you continued your assaults on our persons." Kristain continued down the stairs while Mitch followed toward the door.

"I swear! Not one more scratch, not another cut, no more blood!"

Mitch stopped in his progress toward the door and turned to look at Babbet. The look in his eyes made her cringe.

"Your continued pursuit of your own pleasure at the cost of pain to others will someday be your downfall." Even as he spoke, he remembered the look on her face as she had licked the blood off his brother's hand.

The maniacal smile she had worn when she had first seen the blood made him shudder. And he made sure she saw his disgust run through him as he remembered.

He turned again and looked to his brother. Kristain nodded to him in silent agreement, they weren't the ones to punish this woman.

The brothers went through the door of the splendidly lavish house and heard Babbet, a woman they couldn't imagine as their mate, shriek vile words at them and curse their manhood.

"You'll be back! I swear it! You'll never find another woman to give you what I've been able to! You'll never find another woman who'll take the both of you and give you what I can. The pleasures you've found with me has made you men. You'll only ever be half men until you come back to me! Bastards! What's a little blood between lovers? You liked it! You're just too damn childish to know what it takes to please a woman! Damn you, come back!"

Her sobs and curses droned on until the two men opened their truck doors and climbed in, shutting the doors as if to shut out the relationship they had briefly shared with the woman.

Mitch turned to his brother and with a mental stroke of shared pain and comfort, spoke.

"I'm sorry. I wish somehow we had seen that coming." He reached out and grasped Kristain's shoulder.

Kristain continued to look out the windshield of the truck, but brought his own hand up to join with his brother's. "I know, I know. If we hadn't been so intent on our own pleasures instead of the pursuit for our bride, we both might have seen her for what she was."

When he turned to look at Mitch, a small smile played at his lips. "But remember this, brother mine. We will surely know the woman who is our intended bride when we meet her."

Mitch held out his hand, and Kristain nodded. As they clasped hands, both opened their minds to show that in all things, they trusted each other.

Almost One Year Later

"Wait! Don't move." The woman continued to hold onto Kristain's arm as she scanned the room for her sister. "I know she was talking to—well, I can't remember their names right now, but it was over there near the buffet table."

She finally turned back to Kristain and looked into his eyes imploringly.

"I'm so sorry. I don't mean to keep you, it's just…well, an acquaintance of ours suggested I ask…ummm—" She paused, and stopped completely to look over his shoulder.

Kristain felt Mitch behind him and knew what had made the woman silent. It happened every time a woman laid eyes on the brothers together.

"Hello." Kristain heard Mitch say and knew he could have gotten away from the woman. She reached out her other hand clasping his brother's in welcome while mumbling a hello.

Mitch let go of her hand and turned to his brother. "Are you going to introduce me?"

Kristain smiled. "It seems our reputation has preceded us. This is Jan Armand, and at present, she is looking for her sister. Jan has informed me her sister, Stephanie, has asked her about finding two interested partners for a *ménage à trois*."

Kristain watched as his brother's eyebrows rose and his face took on an intrigued look. In truth, Kristain had sent a call for his brother to come and meet the woman. Now all they needed was to find the actual interested party.

He sidestepped, slightly blocking Jan's view of Mitch, and willed her to focus on him.

It took a few moments, but she finally turned her gaze back to him.

"Do you want to see if you can find her now, or would you rather we planned to meet her some other time?" It took her a few more moments of staring, but she finally shook her head in a negative response.

"No." She looked between the brothers, then once again over her shoulder and started to speak when she turned back to them with a smile on her face. The look was one of a quiet happiness, a look a mother would give a child, or —

Kristain and Mitch turned to look at the same time.

"There she is. There's my sister." Mitch and Kristain both heard the love in Jan's voice as she pointed to where a woman stood with two other men. The three seemed to be in an animated conversation.

Kristain and Mitch felt each other's response and knew they had found their mate.

With their minds linked and their cocks swelled, they felt everything inside which made them who and what they were shout out that they must run, not walk, to claim her.

Kristain both heard and felt the feral growl that escaped his brother and matched it with one of his own. It was all he could do not to go over to the males who surrounded her and stake a very public claim.

Unfortunately, they were on Earth, and the claim he and his brother would have liked to make involved stripping her naked and ramming their cocks into her so deep and so hard they would lose themselves in her essence.

Easy, brother mine, Mitch said as he reached an arm out and grasped Kristain lightly. *I also feel the pull, but we need to be very sure this time.*

Kristain watched as one of the male's face lit up when Stephanie spoke to him. He began to gesture down his own body as if trying to make shapes appear out of thin air. Kristain had to stop himself from striding forward and smashing a fist in the man's face when he reached his hands out to Stephanie and began to draw lines from the shoulders of her dress to her waist.

Out of the corner of his eye, and in the recess of his mind where his brother's presence resided, Kristain both felt and watched as Mitch took one, then another step forward, as if he also had the idea of getting physical with the man.

Have a care brother. Kristain spoke to Mitch in the others mind. *Do not frighten her before she has even had the opportunity to meet us.*

Kristain turned to look into his brother's eyes. *When we finally meet, she will be ours.*

Damn! Mitch thought. She was finally within their grasp and all he could do was stand here and watch as she laughed at something another man said! If it had been up to him, they would have gone to her, explained who they were, and scooped her up with a shouted exclamation she belonged to them, taken her from the room and ravished her in the nearest spot which afforded some privacy!

The thought of what he and Kristain were soon going to do with her had his cock throbbing in time to the beating pulse in his heart.

He wanted badly to stay and find some reason to go to her, but hesitated at the words his brother had spoken in his mind. They didn't want to frighten her off, and if she got one glance at the hard-on he was sporting, she might just run screaming from him!

Mitch gave his brother a nod and mental thanks.

Kristain nodded his head and turned back to Jan.

"She is all you have said. If you would like, we can meet her now and bind—excuse me, I mean find out if she is willing to accept us."

Jan shook her head once, then again, as her gaze found Kristain's once again and she seemed to come to a decision.

"No, I don't think so. She asked me to set it up, and from what I've heard, the two of you...well let's just say I've heard nothing but wonderful things about your characters."

The brothers smiled in unison, and Jan had to lock her knees to keep from falling from the combination the two men made. If she could bottle whatever it was that made these two men shout moresexmoresexmoresex, she would be a rich woman!

Steeling herself against the lust she felt, she turned once again and looked at Stephanie. That was all it took, her mind focused. She was positive these two men were exactly what her sweet, yet daring sister needed.

Her gaze went to Mitch and she turned her own Million-Dollars-Plus-Contract smile on him.

"So long as you two know this—I will eviscerate either of you if you hurt her in any way. Nothing and no one will stop me."

The men quit smiling for a moment, and a serious look came over their faces. Jan watched as each of them put a hand to their hearts, gave a slight bow, then each reached out and took one of her hands.

The brothers spoke in tandem, and their words were formal sounding.

"By the honor you have bestowed on us, may you own our lives and souls should we fail in our promise given to you this day."

Taken aback slightly, yet in no way put off by their words, Jan gave a regal nod of her head.

"Just see that you don't." With that, both men grinned, and Jan smiled in return.

"Now, have you two eaten yet?"

"We thank you for everything, but we have already eaten." Kristain brought Jan's hand to his mouth where he brushed his lips across her knuckles briefly, then released it.

"I'm afraid we've actually stayed longer than we had planned. If you'll call this number, we can set up a time to meet with either you, or both you and your sister." Mitch removed one of the cards they'd had made up a few months ago and handed it to Jan.

Jan took the card, looked it over, and stuck it in the little clutch bag she carried.

"I'll give you a call and we'll have lunch while we discuss the arrangements. How's that sound?" Mitch and Kristain both smiled.

"Just fine." Kristain agreed. "We'll be off now, and it was lovely meeting you." Both brothers turned and made their way toward the entrance they had walked through barely an hour ago.

"So. You think she's the one?" Mitch asked Kristain as they stood outside waiting for the valet to retrieve their truck.

Kristain's answer was immediate.

"You felt the same as I. Our response to her was exactly as it is written of how we know our mates." He paused for a moment then turned his head and looked Mitch directly in the eye.

"Can you stand here and tell me you do not think she is the one?"

Mitch stared back at the one person in all creation he couldn't lie to and gave his brother a slight bow.

"Forgive me? You are right. I do know she's the one, but it doesn't mean she won't be..." His words trailed off as Kristain smiled, then laughed at him.

"Really Mitch! You'll see. When we have her to ourselves, you will know it is right."

Mitch looked from his brother to the truck pulling up, then back to Kristain.

"Fine. I will accept it when we meet her and it is confirmed." The tone of his voice was even, and Kristain knew Mitch had already made up his mind. He was just too stubborn to show it.

The valet got out and looked at the brothers with indecision on her face. But before she could offer the keys to Kristain, Mitch held out his hand, took the keys, gave her a generous tip and walked around to the other side to get in.

Kristain climbed into the passenger's side with a knowing smile and mentally prepared himself for the time when the three of them would finally be together.

* * * * *

Mitch remembered how it all led to this moment, as he and Kristain stepped off the elevator onto the floor where Stephanie lived.

"Remember…" Mitch started, but trailed off when Kristain turned back with a smile.

"Don't worry. She's the one. You know it, I know it, and now we just have to help Stephanie know it." Kristain turned back and looked from his left to his right. He stopped when he found the number he had been looking for and looked down to make sure his clothing was perfect. Happily finding it to be just fine, he looked back at Mitch as he reached out and pressed the button for the doorbell.

"Now stop worrying, and let us go get our mate."

Chapter 2
Inside Stephanie's Apartment

Hearing the doorbell ring, Stephanie got up from the couch, and turned off the television. Checking herself in the mirror on the way to the door, she patted a few flyaway strands of what her father called, her brown-bear-hair and lifted a finger to her full lower lip, wiping away a smudge of lipstick.

A few of the photographers she worked with had offered to practice on her if she could doll herself up. While she had been flattered, she politely declined and went on with whatever task they had needed done. Ah, the days could be long and hard, or long and wonderful, when working in HollyWeird.

The bell sounded again and made her think it was now or never.

Smoothing her skirt and checking her blouse one last time, she walked to her apartment door, took a deep, trembling breath, and opened it.

Two of the most striking and majestic men she had ever seen before stood on the other side. Both looked as if they had just stepped from the covers of GQ magazine.

The pair oozed SEX out of every pore of their bodies.

They were twins no less. A pair of drop dead, 'Oh. My. God. I think I'm going to come', twins. They stood around six foot, three inches tall, silky dark brown hair which fell a few inches below their collared shirts, and bodies to make the Olympian Gods jealous with envy.

Muscles rippled under the silk dress shirts the brothers wore beneath their suit coats and made her mouth water. Her tongue came out of her mouth to make a brief swipe at wetting her lips before she looked further down.

Her eyes locked on rigid twin bulges the brothers sported and her breath went out in a silent sigh of longing. For one long second her head felt light, the world went dark, and she couldn't quite catch her breath.

Finally, taking a much needed breath, she let her gaze wander farther, then looked back up into their faces.

Her inventory couldn't have taken more than a few brief moments, but one of the mens lips twitched as if he held back a sensual smile, while the look in other's eyes could have melted an iceberg.

Blinking rapidly a few times, then focusing on their faces once more, she noticed the only real physical difference between the brothers was the color of their eyes. One had brown eyes, the other blue.

She knew plenty of women who would offer up sacrifices for a few hours of hot sex with either of them. She had gotten luckier than most—she had them both for a whole weekend!

She was going to have a *ménage à trois* with these two magnificent strangers.

Mitch stood staring at the woman he'd only seen from afar, and at this distance he knew their choice was flawless.

She was everything her sister had said and more. The beautiful, luminous skin and luxurious hair, and the smile, which said, "I know what you're thinking, and let's try it."

Jan had commented that although Stephanie had wanted to experiment, she was a little reluctant to go out and find two partners who would indulge her.

Kristain, and Mitch shared a mutual friend with Jan. Jan had called her the sweetest woman she had worked with on one of her catalog shoots. And Mitch would know as, it was through this friend, Jan had learned Mitch and Kristain preferred to be together with the same woman.

Always.

When Jan had approached them, she had done her best to explain what it was her sister had been hoping to experience.

He and Kristain were here to give the shy, yet surprisingly confident sister, exactly what she wanted.

A weekend of uninhibited sex.

Earlier That Week

"Hold still Jan. I need to get this perfect, or Mr. Have No Patience will have us here for another day's shooting. I know how much you want to miss the first vacation you've had in 14 months. Right?"

"All right slave driver." Jan remained still until Steph stepped back from her to critique the application of the newest eye shadow from LaVi Cosmetics.

To Stephanie, this was art. Not to mention her reputation and livelihood.

"Well? Will it do?" Jan sat waiting for the final vote.

"It would if Dirkins wasn't such a perfectionist. Not that I mind so much, but just think about it. The amount of time I've spent in here working on you, I could have spent doing make-up for the entire ensemble of the cast of Cats, and still done the next showing." Stephanie moved in to apply a fresh coat of blusher and again stepped back to look at Jan's make-up critically.

She had the eye and talent to go with it. She was the most sought after make-up artist around. Film, stage, television, even dead celebrities, Steph did them all.

The first time she had done a "Dead Celebrity", one particularly inebriated mourner had gone up to the coffin and told the deceased to get up and get his ass back on the set. Enough was enough, and he had won the bet between them.

Of course the corpse had just lain there still—and dead! The mourner had broken down and sobbed all the harder after being told his best friend really was dead, and it wasn't a joke.

"He's really dead? Gone? No more hanging from the chandeliers?" The man had sobbed harder still.

"You bastard! Why did you leave me?!?" Eventually, he had to be sedated to make it through the remainder of the service.

Not only could she make dead people look alive, she could make living people look believably dead. She had won numerous awards, and so far, two Oscars. She had an affinity for her work. When clients came to her giving descriptions of what they wanted, or what they were looking for in a character, it was as if she read their minds. It was why she had become so popular in her craft, and why she was too quickly burning out. Lately, she wasn't having nearly as much fun being at the head of the business.

Applying blusher with a deft hand, Stephanie spoke.

"You know, if we hadn't been related, I wouldn't put up with Dirkins at all. This is one of the last shoots I'll personally be doing."

Jan studied Steph almost as critically as Steph had evaluated Jan's make-up.

"And you know I adore you for it." Jan spoke around the lip brush Stephanie wielded. "But I've been noticing for a while you've been at odds with your love of the craft. You've only been going through the motions, haven't you?"

"Unfortunately, yes, and I've noticed it in my work. The creative side is still a dream, but the people I've been dealing with…" Stephanie shook her head.

"Not for anything will I do another shoot with Dirkins or another of his type. The man is a…" She wasn't going there.

"Besides, Cathy's been chomping at the bit to 'step up to the challenge' as she's so boldly put it, and I'm all for giving her the chance to take over more of the productions. She deserves it. She's damn good."

Jan smiled.

"So take a little time off and see if that helps. Plus, you've still got one more thing on your to-do list."

Stephanie focused intently on Jan and sighed, shaking her head.

"I know, but let's focus on this shoot right now. I don't think your make-up could get any more perfect if you had it surgically implanted to come out of your pores. Not that Dirkins will appreciate it, but you're done." She walked over to her many cases and started to put away a few of the things she wouldn't need again.

"Steph, *are* you still serious about what we talked about the other day?" Jan asked as she pulled off the smock draped over her costume. Standing carefully, she turned to look Steph straight in the eyes and did her best not to blink too much before the eye make-up dried.

Stephanie looked up at Jan and opened her mouth to say no. "Of course." Startled that what she had meant to say hadn't come out of her mouth, she looked at her own reflection in the mirror and then swung sharply back to Jan.

Jan came over to the mirror and studied her face just as critically as Stephanie had.

"Damn you're good! I can't ever get my face to look like this. And I'm glad you're still serious because Joe and Jim Bob said to meet them at their trailer where you could start to rockin' it as soon as you walked through the door." Jan said all this as she bent to pickup her scarf and drape it over her hair.

Startled, Steph's head snapped around to stare straight into Jan's laughing eyes.

Giggling, Jan patted Stephanie's shoulder affectionately. "Really, woman. If I knew you wouldn't make me sit here for another two and a half hours to redo my face, I'd laugh until I cried. That was a priceless expression. I'm going to capture it on camera some day."

Sighing shakily, Stephanie blew out a relieved breath. "So long as you were only kidding about the trailer. And you know it's not because I wouldn't go for a man who lived in a trailer park, because obviously," a look of fear passed through her eyes, "I would. I just don't need that kind of housing right now."

Jan gave Steph a quick hug, the equivalent to a bear hug in the fashion industry, except their bodies hardly contacted at all.

"Okay. No talking about Rob—you know who." When Jan looked at Stephanie, she wore a grateful look, "or where he lived."

"So then, I called two guys I know who are dying to get you in the sack with them. They know what they're doing and both want to please you in anyway they can in hopes it won't be a one time thing."

Picking up the umbrella she had been using until the actual shooting started, Jan headed for the make-up trailer's door.

"Their names are Mitch and Kristain and they know you as Sunshine." Jan fiddled with her scarf to make sure it wouldn't brush make-up from her face. "I have to get to the set. They may be paying me $6,000.00 an hour, but it doesn't mean I have to become known as the woman who drags her feet in order to get more money out of them." Looking back in the mirror as she went down the steps to see if she had ruined the line of the dress, she stopped short, shook her head, and looked back at her sister.

"Almost forgot. Me being a blonde and all, I know it isn't that unusual."

Stephanie laughed at their running inside joke knowing Jan was the last blonde in the world who was anything close to stereotypical.

"What?" Stephanie continued gathering used tissues and wiping up the little bits of make-up she had knocked over.

"Well, not to be a pain in the ass, but I told both Mitch and Kristain they should be at your apartment after dark, and preferably late on Friday." Knowing she might just get a serious kick in the butt for it, Jan hurriedly went on with her confession.

Making sure she was next to the exit. See, no dim-witted blonde here. Taking a deep breath, she told Steph the rest.

"I also told them not to bother to pack more than a toothbrush and a few play toys." Hurriedly, Jan went on before Stephanie could open her mouth.

"And when you were on your way to the set today, and I told you I'd needed to take my car because I had a few stops before the shoot? I stocked your apartment with a few odds and ends I knew you didn't have. Have a good time. I love you."

With that, Jan raced out the door.

Stephanie Louise Armand stared after her sister, one Janice Luellen. She wanted to fume, but she knew it was a study in futility.

Again a sigh escaped her throat, but this time there were nerves in it. She sat down and looked at herself in the mirror. Even to her she looked scared. Dammit! She was a grown woman, and she was going to do this! Fear or no fear, deep down inside, her loins were screaming about enjoying it more than either of the two men would.

Much more.

Back at Stephanie's Apartment Door

Stephanie opened the door a little wider and stepped forward with what she hoped was a sensual smile. She wondered if either of them noticed how badly she was shaking. Then she wondered how they couldn't.

She held out her hand to the man nearest her and looked into his warm brown eyes. He looked down at her outstretched hand and brought his larger one up to meet hers. Stephanie followed his movement and looked down. For some reason her eyes locked onto the size of his fingers.

Keeping the smile on as best she could, Stephanie tried to banish the images of just what those large, thick fingers could do for her. Looking up again, she saw she might not be the only one who was thinking such thoughts.

The man's eyes had gone from warm to sizzling, while lightning bolts stormed in them.

He held onto her hand as he spoke.

"Are we to assume you are Sunshine Armand, and you assume who we are? Or would you rather we introduce ourselves?" Even as he said it, his eyes held both fire and laughter. Stephanie damn near melted at his feet right there.

Taking a deep breath, she rearranged her smile into some semblance of what she hoped was slightly worldly and sophisticated.

She would get through her apprehension.

She hoped.

Chapter 3

Kristain stood holding onto Stephanie's hand and smiled even larger inside. His mind linked to Mitch's and he spoke. *Now, did I not reassure you she would be worthy of being our mate and the mother of our children?*

Watching Mitch out of the corner of his eye, he saw his brother look closely at Stephanie Armand and heard him admit there wasn't a better choice in the universe. All that was left was to convince her of it.

Yes. She will be treasured beyond our mother, grandmother, and their sisters ever were. Now, if you would allow us to be invited in so the wooing and consummating could start, I'd appreciate it. I'm hard as a zarsus, and ready for this marriage to begin.

Of course. Shall we? Kristain brought Stephanie's hand to his lips and, turning it over to expose her palm, bent and raked his teeth gently over the pad at the base of her thumb.

Shivering, Stephanie closed her eyes and lost the smile she had been holding desperately onto. Slowly opening her eyes, she gazed into heated, brown eyes. Clearing her throat of the lust choking her, it took her three tries to get the words out.

"Of course. How thoughtless of me. I'm Ste…Sunshine Armand, and you would be?" She hoped they hadn't noticed her stumble, and tried to take her hand back, but he gripped it with a gentle and easy strength.

"I am Kristain. Both my brother and I have been admiring you greatly since Jan pointed you out to us at a party we all attended. It is an honor to accept the privilege of your gift."

Stephanie looked into his eyes and barely heard anything he'd said beyond his name. Oh, she knew he was talking, but the words had no meaning beyond sound.

Noticing his lips had stopped moving, even though he continued to smile at her, she nodded her head and hoped whatever he had said hadn't involved something painful.

He turned to the other gentleman and seemed to transfer her hand to his in a way that allowed them all to maintain contact for a brief moment.

She felt a jolt of…well, the best she could come up with was power, go through her hand and travel up her arm until it seemed to fill her whole body. Gasping, she stared at the other man, Mitch. He must be Mitch. He had her hand gripped in his; again, it was a gentle yet firm hold.

Looking from one man to the other, her perception of the two as separate beings changed. Apart they were phenomenal, together, they were devastatingly, utterly, *male*. The two were obviously twins, so very much alike, yet upon closer inspection different as night and day. Seeing them now while each held her hand, Stephanie found they complimented each other in a way she never thought possible.

Mitch spoke, snapping Stephanie back to herself.

"I am Mitch. As Kristain has stated, I too am honored to be your chosen."

He brought her hand to his lips, also turning her hand palm up and biting the pad of her thumb gently.

She stared into his eyes and saw the same lust-filled smile as Kristain's eyes had held.

Kristain cleared his throat, making Stephanie shake her head to clear the thoughts she had seen swimming within Mitch's blue eyes.

"Sunshine?" He paused to frown slightly. "Is this your true name?"

Mitch let go of her hand and Stephanie forced herself not to cradle it next to her heart. It still felt as if both men were holding it in their joined hands. Shaking her head in the negative, she blurted out her real name.

"No, it's Stephanie."

It was her turn to frown. Now why had she admitted that? She had meant to answer only to Sunshine all weekend. They shouldn't know her true name, as when in the business world, she went by Sunshine. She looked between the two and noticed there was yet another question on their faces.

"What?" Even to her it sounded defensive, but she felt as if they were reproaching her, even while their smiles stayed in place.

Mitch spoke this time.

"It's a lovely name and I prefer it to Sunshine. But I was wondering—" He paused slightly and looked into her apartment behind her.

Stephanie blushed slightly. If they hadn't been staring so hard at her, she would have smacked herself in the forehead in a stupid me gesture.

"Sorry, I…umm, won't you come in?" she gestured behind her.

Smiling as if they thought her amusing, both men waited right where they were.

"You don't want to come in?" She watched as the brother's eyebrows raised simultaneously at her question. "What? Are we going to do this right here in the hall?"

Even as the words came out of her mouth, she wanted to snatch them back. The men had turned to each other and burst into simultaneous laughter.

Stephanie closed her eyes and her head lowered slightly toward her chest. She wanted to turn around and shut the door on them. She realized they couldn't come in because she was still blocking the door.

Wondering if she could just close the door and start over, she backed into the apartment, gesturing lamely for the two, who were still chuckling, to enter. Okay, so she was nervous as hell. How was she going to pull off any kind of sophisticated poise with these two divine specimens of walking, talking, breathing…sex gods?

I knew she was the one. A sense of humor and a sense of naiveté. She is scared beyond her comprehension; yet still aching with a need I have never felt in a woman. She practically screams with want for the two of us.

Knowing this phenomenon wasn't all that unusual, Kristain could still feel what his brother meant.

The woman he walked past had a longing he ached to fill. She didn't want this only for herself, he realized. Her mind fairly screamed with the need to share in her pleasure.

Kristain was picking up her surface thoughts rather easily. He now knew she was thirty. She had achieved most of her life goals. But a trip to a NASA space camp and a swim through alligator infested waters was now feeling less fearsome than sex with him and Mitch.

His eyes widened as he discovered she had actually studied up on having multiple partners. He wanted to delve into a little more of her thoughts, and then he swore he wouldn't intrude any longer until invited. She was not to be some casual partner. He needed to respect her mind.

Mitch interrupted his thoughts and stated the obvious for both of them in a growling thought. *She might have studied up on multiple partners, but we will be the only 'multiple' she'll ever get.*

Kristain emphatically nodded as he tuned back in to what Stephanie was saying.

"…tea, and don't go for the old 'or me' line. I'm only offering you a drink if you'd like one." This was said with a slight smile on her face, which turned into a shy look as she looked down at the floor rather than at them.

Speaking softly, she lifted her eyes to look up through her eyelashes, in a more bashful than flirtatious way, and ended saying softly, "After all, I've already offered myself to you both, and since you're both here, obviously my invitation was accepted."

Did I just say that? Stephanie thought, wanting to run into her room and lock the door. Flames of embarrassment crawled up her face and heated her cheeks.

Maybe she should only open her mouth for yes or no questions, or for specifically asked questions. Ones like, Do you enjoy me doing this here? How about here? Questions that would keep her from wanting to sink through the floor from mortification.

Stop it! She admonished herself. You wanted this, and the only way to get it is to do it. She could do this. It couldn't be harder than any other new experience.

Could it?

We must put her at ease. Kristain said to Mitch.

What would you like me to start with? How about an orgasm from her just standing and wondering how this is going to work?

Kristain walked toward Stephanie and reached out to stroke her cheek.

"Do not be afraid, cherished one. We will do all we can to put you at your ease. We will give you pleasure and worship your body as it was intended to be." Even as he said the words, Stephanie seemed to relax.

In truth, relaxed wasn't the right word. It was more of a bone melting attributed to the deep baritone voice pouring out words. She knew she should understand him, but all her brain heard were body throbbing vibrations from his voice.

She stood straight, with her arms down at her sides, and looked up into those brown eyes again. She felt as if she could orgasm right here.

Shaking her head mentally she thought it just might clue the two of them in to the fact it had been—a while.

Pushing off of the couch he'd been leaning on, Mitch decided it was time to "surround" her with their presence. He didn't want to rush her—

Okay, so he did want to rush her, but he didn't want to scare her. He wanted to make her more comfortable around them. After all, they would be spending the rest of their lives in bed together.

He smiled thinking the thought held definite appeal to him.

To be trapped in a bed with Stephanie, himself, and Kristain for life. With nothing but heated bodies and the pungent scent of sex and sweat to feed them into a frenzy of lustful fucking? Oh yeah! He really didn't think Kristain would argue with the setting either.

Kristain let his eyelids slip another notch when he noticed the glow around Stephanie's head, then groaned in ecstasy at the thoughts coming from his brother's mind. He wanted to reach down and stroke his cock, then pull Stephanie's hand down to join him in his explorations.

Soon, it will be soon. Kristain spoke both to himself, and his brother as Mitch walked around to come up behind Stephanie. Out of the corner of his eye, Kristain saw as the shudder raced through Mitch. Kristain experienced the miracle of a twins' true mate and their three-way mental link as he shared the sensations Stephanie and Mitch were feeling as well as their thoughts. It was everything he'd been told, and more.

Mitch placed his hands on either side of her slender, yet voluptuous waist, and began to lightly knead her hips. She was startled at first, but soon reveled in his added touch.

He aligned their bodies and let her feel his cock against her ass while he began to widen the areas he touched.

"Hmmm…I…I guess this means—" She paused as Kristain's left hand swept down her face leaving a path of goose bumps from her neck on, until his hand was feathering gently over her right breast.

Mitch spoke softly into her left ear. "What does this mean?"

One hand stroked up her left side, where he flitted his fingers faintly across her left nipple.

Stephanie trembled in their grasp and tried to remember what she had been about to say.

"Ummm…ohhh…dr…dr…drink—" She struggled with the thought as the men chose that moment to each firmly grasp a breast and pinch a nipple.

Mitch continued his assault on her left breast as he whispered.

"Why thank you. I'd love to have a sip of you." Turning Stephanie's head toward her left side with his right hand, he brushed his lips caressingly across hers once, then again. He dropped his hand to her side as he began to stroke her right buttock.

Her lips stayed as much in contact with Mitch's as she could get them.

Another set of lips and a tongue swept over the other side of her throat where her neck was exposed. She quivered with the awareness traveling through her body.

All thoughts, with the exception of a select few, flew right out of her head. One of her thoughts that stayed just happened to be, *God, please don't let them stop!*

Kristain raised his head a little and whispered ever so softly in her ear. "Never," then continued his assault on the very sensitive bend in her neck.

Mitch seemed to be enjoying her lips. His tongue came out to sweep across her lips and taste them as if the peach wine she had been sipping before they arrived still lingered in her mouth.

Biting at her lip with just the right amount of pressure to have her open her mouth for him, Mitch swept his tongue over the hurt to soothe it and let his tongue glide into her mouth to find the even stronger taste of peaches on her tongue. It was a light and questing touch he used to explore her mouth, as if he wanted to imprint her taste and texture on his being.

Stephanie felt Kristain move from her neck and breast and slide to his knees. He leaned his head into her stomach, and turning to the side, he rubbed his cheek over her blouse. He must have felt he wasn't close enough, because he sat back on his heels, and tugged the blouse out of the top of her skirt and raised it up.

Leaning back into her stomach, he rubbed his warm, smooth cheek against her bare skin. She looked down as best she could to see heat flare into his eyes.

Stephanie felt as if she had been dipped into some kind of vat of Sensitize-Your-Body gel. Every millimeter of her skin was on fire. The places either of the men touched burned and made heat flare inside her. Soon, her legs wouldn't hold her. They felt like Jell-O and probably quivered just as badly.

Kristain's arms were under her skirt doing things to her thighs which made her want to lie down and open them wider. His hands traced over her French cut silk panties in patterns designed to drive her crazy, but had no rhyme or reason to them.

She didn't care. She was already closer to an orgasm than she had ever been in her life and if either one of them pushed a little further—

Stephanie threw back her head and screamed.

Kristain deftly pushed her skirt up to her hips and pulled the side of her panties out, tucking them along the fold of her leg. He leaned into her body at her crotch and breathed gently on her pussy. Even more heat adding to an already raging inferno. Leaning in even further, he used one hand to part her nether lips and flicking his tongue out, scraped it across her clit.

The action sent her into another scream. He still had his arms wrapped around her thighs and held her in place to suckle gently on her clitoris.

She continued to scream.

Kristain's eyes began to bleed into the color of gold as he thought of the hours, days, years of pleasure this responsive woman would give him and Mitch. At this moment, it took all his control not to spread her legs further and ram his pulsing cock into her cunt.

A stray thought flitted through his mind of both Mitch's and his sons lying in her womb. First they would each give her a set of twins. Soon though, she would give them an empire.

But this would be the mother of his children, and he wouldn't treat her like other women he and Kristain had shared over the centuries.

At least not until she asked them to!

"Thank you, Stephanie." Kristain got to his feet and gave Stephanie a light peck on the cheek. He was rock-hard and his cock strained against his pants as if it was trying to escape.

Which it was.

"You are a wonderful hostess to provide a guest with such a delightful appetizer."

Stephanie's head rested on Mitch's shoulder. She was positive she couldn't move. If this was only a preview of what was to come—oops—giggling shakily, she thought of the unintended pun she had just imagined.

Mitch's hands still made intriguing forays along her body while he spoke softly into her ear.

"So glad to have amused you. Anything else we can do for you?"

Still giggling, Stephanie reclined the rest of the way on Mitch and took him at his word.

"Since you asked—" How could she still be shy after what she had just done, she thought to herself.

Kristain's lips showed a faint trace of a smile. He didn't want to openly grin like a fool at her, although it wouldn't take much for that to happen. As he stood up, and Stephanie reveled in orgasmic aftermath, he noticed Mitch ridding her of her skirt. He wondered quite frankly if she had noticed it.

Not that it mattered at this moment. They were going to strip her naked and do wonderful things to her anyway.

He felt as if a hand squeezed his shaft with the pressure of a vise. He longed to ride the feeling to orgasm, but restrained himself.

"It is your fantasy, what do you wish?" Kristain's growled.

"Ummm…ummm…I can't…think…Mitch—" Stephanie was going back up the crest toward orgasm. Surely there was no way she could have another one this quick.

Could she?

"Don't think. Just feel." Mitch had grasped her panties from behind and was sawing them back and forth over her clitoris.

"Yes—feel." Kristain ground his bulging hard-on into her crotch.

"But…you said…nuhhh…want…ohhh—" She both wanted to shout at them to stop what they were doing and beg them to never stop.

They had asked what she wanted them to do to her. Both were doing just fine right now. She could always make a list later, maybe.

"Yes, I do want." Kristain's voice vibrated through her body. She was positive he spoke only into her ear, but she could feel every word strumming through her nerve endings.

"I want, too. We both want what you can give. Will you allow us to give you more?" Kristain trailed his hands down her breast as Mitch's hands gripped the inside of her thighs and began kneading them.

"Will you allow us to pleasure you more? We will do as you say. Whatever you wish of us." Mitch moved his hands to the bend in her legs and began to use the outsides of his fingers to skim along the outside of her nether lips.

He wanted to plunge his fingers in her drenched pussy but held back to wait for her permission.

It was custom to ask for entry into your soon-to-be-wife's body. He would do nothing to mar the chance of her acceptance when they returned home.

Mitch wanted it imbedded in her mind she had given her consent. There would be no scandal surrounding their house.

Both men waited for permission.

Stephanie felt their gazes as if they tried to burn it into her skin. She opened her eyes with difficulty and gazed into a pair of golden eyes. Hadn't Kristain's eyes been a very deep brown before?

Mitch seemed to read her mind as he brushed his mouth across her cheek while reaching his other hand around to cup her pussy.

Thought went out of her head and he eased up so she could give an answer.

Kristain banked the fire raging in his body so his eyes bled back into their normal brown. He knew eventually she would see them bleed back into gold and shimmer when he reached his orgasm, but for now it was best to leave that fact to be found out when they brought her to orgasm together.

Stephanie's thoughts seemed to coalesce into some semblance of order when Mitch let up on his assault of her senses and realized it was time to move this party to a flat surface so she could lie down.

If they didn't, she would collapse.

No sooner had she the thought than Mitch moved his hands and swung her up into his arms.

She felt the thick muscles bulge and flex as he easily held her. She wouldn't have thought so much muscle was hidden behind the dress shirt he wore. She wondered if Kristain and Mitch were equally matched twins all over their bodies. Then realized she would find out soon.

Looking toward Mitch, she noticed his blue eyes had darkened. Opening her mouth to speak was a challenge while gazing at the hunger in those eyes.

"I...ummm...are you ready to—" Mitch gave Stephanie a questioning look at her hesitation.

Swallowing all the lust once more, she tried again. "The bedroom?" this time she made it a question.

"Wherever you wish us to go. Lead and we shall follow."

Carte blanche! Where had Jan found these two demi-gods? What she wouldn't have given for these two before she'd met—

Don't think about it! Don't! Stephanie firmly reminded herself. All it will lead you to is pain and fear, and those emotions have no place here and now.

Feeling her stiffen slightly in his arms, Mitch read her thoughts to make sure it had nothing to do with him, and asked his brother. *She has been...what is the word? Help me Kristain.* Mitch was angered by the pain, rage, and helplessness that had just come from Stephanie.

She has been used and...stalked I believe the word is. Kristain had come up to stroke a hand down her cheek and cupped it to comfort her.

"Easy. We'll go as slow as you need."

Smiling at the reassurance and the feeling of Mitch's grip tightening his hold on her, Stephanie gathered herself and blew out a calming breath. She would leave all that behind right now. It didn't belong between the three of them, period.

"Thank you both."

"Lead and we will follow."

Stephanie, choosing to take his meaning literally, directed him.

"If you go down the hall right there, my bedroom is at the end." Pointing to the hallway, she then tucked her hand back between Mitch's body and hers.

She was ready for this. Her mama might have told her good girls don't, but Stephanie was sure mama had lied through her teeth!

Mitch carried her down the hallway, with Kristain trailing behind, and entered into her bedroom where she immediately noticed one of the gifts her sister had left.

Right there on her headboard were three of the largest boxes of condoms she had ever seen in her life! They said party pack and looked to have more than one of a kind. The box nearest to her said something about flavors and tasty treats. Her face flamed as she read the next one. Glow-in-the-dark, ribbed, thin, horse hung, choco-choco-nuts. The list seemed to go on.

But the most embarrassing part of it was the little note beside the first box in her sister's block letter handwriting.

In bold capital letters, it read:

The other 12 boxes are in the bathroom.

If you need more than this, be sure and document it!

Even as she read it Kristain's chuckles could be heard from beside her and she felt more than heard the laughter coming from Mitch.

Sighing at her sister's antics, she wondered how many more surprises they would find over the weekend.

Looking down at the corner of her bed where something had caught her eye, she saw what she could swear was a strap of leather with fur on the inside. It took her a moment more to realize what it was.

"Restraints," she mumbled, turning so her face was partially hidden in Mitch's shoulder.

She was going to kill her sister—just as soon as they tried out those intriguing cuffs!

Chapter 4

Mitch set Stephanie on her feet while still keeping hold of her. She stumbled slightly and used his hold to steady herself.

He had to grin at the stunned look on her face. He wasn't in the least surprised to find Jan had already set the place up. He smiled when he remembered the chat that he, Kristain, and Jan had had before this weekend.

Shaking his head at the luck he and Kristain had stumbled upon by befriending Jan, he looked around.

Hadn't she seen it earlier?

"Did you not know what your sister has gifted you with?" Mitch questioningly teased her.

"Actually—" She paused and bit her lower lip. Should she confess? Shrugging, she let him have a little of the truth.

"Um…I was a tad bit nervous about the two of you…no, the three of us and the new…" she paused as if looking for a specific word to use, "experience. Yes, a new experience, I was going to have…no, we were going to have," she prayed she wasn't blushing as hard as she thought she was.

"Er…I…ummm—" Deciding to just blurt it out, she went on in a rush. "You see, I made up the room so I would feel comfortable and didn't come into it again because I was afraid I would then chicken out."

There. The truth was out.

Although she wasn't nervous now, and in fact was quite relaxed after the lovely orgasm. Her body had quieted down a bit, yet she still felt the humming the two men had brought to life flowing through her nerve endings.

Stephanie knew Kristain had followed them to the room, but as she stood there talking to Mitch, she wondered where he had gone.

She didn't have to wonder long.

Mitch stopped talking abruptly and was looking over her shoulder toward the bathroom. His eyes crinkled and his smile was pure laughter with no sound.

She turned to see what had caught his eye and found Kristain completely naked with gadgets in both hands.

It was her turn to be wide-eyed and open-mouthed. She noticed Kristain was naked and had a massive erection, but what held her astonishment were the items he was displaying.

She had seen them in some catalogues Jan had lent her, and at one time had circled them as if making a wish list of what she found intriguing.

She hadn't been entirely sure at the time she would ever have any use for them, so she had given the catalogues back to her sister and forgotten about them. If she remembered correctly, these particular toys were from Hedonistic Titillaters.

She finally noticed her jaw was inches from the floor and shut her gaping mouth. She blinked and finally looked at Kristain's body rather than what he held.

Before she had seen more than the sculpted chest and chiseled abs, Kristain spoke.

"I do believe I'd like to start with you a lot less clothed and a little wetter. If you'll be so good as to step over here to the bathroom, I think I have a way for you to stay upright."

Mitch stepped up close to her and again rumbled into her ear.

"You will enjoy this immensely. Please," he gently rid her of the garment and laid his warm palm along her waist, then gave her an encouraging push, "trust us. We would never hurt you, and will always keep you safe."

Stephanie barely paused as she went to Kristain. Her steps were sure as again she studied what he had in his hands. This led her line of sight to his enormous erection. It was a work of art. It was no less than eight inches in length, thicker than her forearm, and seemed to be straining to reach his forehead.

She wanted to reach her hands out and see if it was as silky soft as it looked. She must have made a whimpering sound because when she stopped in front of him, he immediately shushed her.

"Not only will it fit, but it won't hurt you at all. We will give you pleasures of which you have never dreamed."

She stared at his penis and wanted to drop to the floor in front of him and give it a thorough inspection. Sounds behind her distracted her though.

She looked over her shoulder to see Mitch calmly stepping out of his underwear and starting for the buttons on his shirt. She watched until he finally slipped the shirt from his shoulders.

When Mitch finished, he left his clothes where they lay and looked into Stephanie's eyes. He smiled again laughingly and she realized her mouth had been hanging open again.

He had to be as close to, if not in fact was, Kristain's size, everywhere!

She turned back at the sound of Kristain clearing his throat.

"Are you all right?" Kristain noticed the deer-caught-in-the-headlights-look. They had shocked her. He started to drop the toys he'd found when she spoke up.

"Sorry." Stephanie shook her head as if it would help. "It's just—well—" She gestured toward Kristain, and then behind her toward Mitch.

He had come up behind her silently and she would have smacked him in the face if he hadn't snapped his head toward the side.

She sighed, and it sounded as if she was overwhelmed. "I have never seen such male perfection outside of a Hollywood shoot. You guys should have come labeled with a warning."

Perfection? She thinks we are perfection, Brother mine. Kristain thought. *If she thinks we are perfection, what will she think when she meets Vincent and Shan Lin?*

Smiling, in what he thought was modesty but was closer to the look the wolf gave Red Riding Hood, Kristain gave a slight bow.

"Thank you. I am grateful we meet with your approval." Kristain said as he led Stephanie into the bathroom.

He laid the restraints, pearled anal beads, and strawberry slather on the vanity table. Stephanie's eyes followed his movements to the table and found they weren't the only things there.

Her sister must have spent a couple thousand dollars filling her wish list from the circled items. There were enough "toys" to last the weekend and then some. She looked beyond them and found they were everywhere.

There were hand and ankle restraints in all shapes and sizes ranging from fur covered to thick leather straps that looked as if they could hold down an entire fleet of bodies. Clamps for the female clitoris and nipples, dildos for both vaginal and anal penetration, and vibrators for both inside and outside stimulation of the female anatomy.

Ben Wah balls in several sizes, lingerie to titillate any man's desires as well as novelty items designed to perk up a dull afternoon. One in particular happened to be the glow-in-the-dark panty and bra set with accompanying glow-in-the-dark condoms.

But the *coup de grâce* in the bathroom had to be what Stephanie could only term as The Portable Jungle Gym. There had to be at least seven different ways to "strap" someone to the thing. She wondered if the boys wouldn't mind trying out all of them with her.

Kristain watched as Stephanie surveyed the equipment.

Jan had bought the full model from one of the S&M clubs in the city and had said she got such a great deal she had it made portable.

Seeing the wide-eyed fascinated look on Stephanie's face made Kristain's already engorged cock jump and begin to throb as if it were begging. He wondered how offended Stephanie would be if he just snatched her to him, strapped her on the Jungle Gym, and pumped them both to an orgasm?

Mitch's voice broke into his thoughts. *I for one won't argue with it, but she has to consent to the first penetration, or there will be no bride.*

You think it's going to be a problem once we get her strapped to the thing? I mean the consent. If I am reading her correctly, she is wondering why we haven't just strapped her in yet. Kristain watched his brother as they spoke together reading Stephanie, and saw in Mitch's reaction he was close to losing all control and taking what he wanted.

Guide her to it and see what happens. We can have her so hot she's agreeing to anything we want to do to her, Kristain looked at Mitch who nodded. *It wouldn't be the first time. And pray gods it won't be the last time with her!*

As both of the men seemed to be in a type of trance, Stephanie walked up to the gym and began to examine it closely.

There, right at the top of both sides, were wrist restraints and—yep, the other ones actually said ankle restraints!

Stephanie thought about this for a moment and then reached up to gently pull on the bar going across the top. She followed the sides with her eyes, rather than her hands, and found there was a way you could actually move the whole contraption into a different position!

She imagined herself strapped to the restraints, butt end up with a man between her legs and one at her mouth.

She closed her eyes as a tiny sound escaped and realized she was even wetter than before.

While Kristain rearranged the settings, Mitch reached for a condom from the bathroom counter and rolled it on. Next he again positioned himself behind her and placed one arm around her left side to clasp his hand around her breast and the other around her waist and then down to her curls where his fingers found her.

Finding her panties still on and in his way, Mitch made quick work of ridding her of them. With a deft tug, he ripped one side, then quickly took care of the other, sliding the thin piece of material out of the way.

Stephanie gave a sigh of relief as cool air settled on her bared skin. Once again she leaned back into Mitch and this time wiggled her naked ass against his straining cock.

Mitch groaned silently and half walked, half danced with Stephanie to where Kristain was loosening the restraints.

He ground his thriving shaft into the slit of Stephanie's buttocks and bent her at the waist while Kristain gently guided her wrists to the cuffs.

When he had them where he wanted, Kristain bent down to kiss Stephanie on the hair. He stroked her hair lovingly and lifted his head to grin at Mitch.

Mitch was rubbing his shaft gently over Stephanie's slit. Up and down and barely coming in contact with where she wanted it to be. If he didn't stop—

"Oh sweet Jesus! Please—"

Moaning in pleasure, Stephanie waited with bated breath for his penetration. When it didn't come and she couldn't stand it any longer, she turned away from admiring Kristain's beautiful manhood from so close a view.

Turning her head to look over her shoulder as best she could, Stephanie watched Mitch stroke his shaft a couple of times as if asking did she want it. She lifted her head a little higher and looked into his eyes with what she was sure had to be a plea of desperation and wondered why he couldn't see it.

"You must invite us in." Turning her head back around, she found Kristain kneeling so he was even with her head and she didn't have to strain.

"What? Are you guys Vampires or something?" She asked in a voice choking with lust.

Kristain's lusty chuckle sent a wave of heat scorching down to her belly, sure she would come right then.

"We will certainly suck you dry, but we have a different way to do it that doesn't involve blood. The taste to us however is still the nectar of our gods. If you will consent, we will be your slaves for eternity." Mitch bowed over her back and bit gently on her neck. Almost as a wolf would do with its mate.

Another sensation flowed into her belly, one of possession. She wanted these two men right now more than she wanted her next breath of air. Eternity would be a tad long, but it would sure be a wild ride! Besides, she was sure he was just using an expression.

Kristain and Mitch looked at each other again, then turned back to Stephanie.

"It is your choice, Stephanie. But we need an answer before we take this any further." Kristain murmured in her ear.

Stephanie could only think of two things at this moment. One, she wanted to taste the cock Kristain had not too long ago put centimeters from her face. Two being the desire to have Mitch sink in so deep she wouldn't know where she began and he ended.

And she wanted it RIGHT NOW!

She opened her mouth to tell them exactly that but it barely came out a croak. She spoke as few words as possible.

"I want you both inside nooow!" The last came out is a guttural growl.

Stephanie wanted to be shocked, acting as if she was a possessed woman. But no sooner had she thought it than she felt Mitch guide the head of his penis to her opening and thrust hard enough to bring her off her feet.

He stayed buried to the hilt inside her tight cunt and gritted his teeth to keep from pumping his come into her.

Kristain sucked in his breath at the feelings coming from his brother. He was waiting until Stephanie could take a breath deeper than a heaving pant before slipping his cock into the velvety heat of her mouth. He didn't know how much longer he could wait, now that he was dealing with Mitch's sensations, too.

Stephanie slowly came back to herself and noticed Mitch was gently thrusting in and out. She opened her eyes, unaware she had closed them.

She looked into Kristain's eyes and noticed he seemed to be awaiting her permission also. She nodded and breathed a yes even as she moaned in unison with the sensations Mitch was giving her.

She felt a satiny soft touch at her lips and stuck out the tip of her tongue in a questing foray, dabbing at the object and hearing an indrawn breath. Smiling to herself and snaking her tongue out a bit farther to lick the head of Kristain's pulsing cock, she laved at it, learning the taste of him.

Giving a few more unhurried explorations with her tongue as she savored the salty sweet flavor before opening her mouth and taking him as deep as she could while feeling Mitch begin to pick up his pace, Stephanie marveled at the unique taste of the man.

Mitch shafted her faster and faster and as his pace quickened, so did her own. She had fantasized about a moment like this. If she hadn't been so—distracted, she would have wondered if the boys had read her mind.

It was her last thought as she exploded and took both men with her. Immense striations of pleasure snaked throughout her body vibrating and scoring her unused muscles as the orgasm broke over her. Stephanie rode through the ecstasy with no thought to it ending, only wallowing in the sheer rapture of the moment.

Kristain watched as Mitch wrapped Stephanie's legs around his waist and held her suspended so Kristain could uncuff her hands from the bars.

He still throbbed and knew it would be another hour before Mitch gave up his position. He didn't mind. His turn was coming. Literally!

Mitch felt the satiny touch of Stephanie's legs around his hips and could have pumped them both to another orgasm in mere moments. But he sensed she needed a position a little more upright at the moment.

He gently helped Kristain prop her up so her head rested on his shoulder once again and gave her a gentle kiss. This one would know only gentleness if he could help it. He'd wrap her in the finest silks and satins and pad every surface she had to walk on with downy feathers and furred rugs.

She would be theirs, and nothing would ever harm her. He knew she would find out soon enough they were very serious indeed. They would mate for life.

Stephanie gratefully accepted the help she got to prop herself up. She knew if Mitch put her down now she would fall flat on her face. Her rubber-for-legs wouldn't allow her to stand.

Stephanie had never had an orgasm anywhere comparable to the one she'd just been given. Even knowing it was selfish, she still prayed the next one would be equal to or better than her last!

Chapter 5

A little while later, Stephanie lay back against the wall, with her legs hanging over the dresser's edge, trying to suck in breath through a parched and rasping throat. She watched as Kristain and Mitch, barely winded, arranged pillows on the bed.

In the last hour or so, the two men had changed positions on the gym, taken Stephanie over the vanity, and now were moving their little group toward the bed.

The last coupling, on the very dresser where she now sat, had been a fast ride up the scale of climax and ended in her screaming loud enough to have her neighbor calling to see if she was all right.

Breathless and not a little proud of herself, she had reassured the sweet woman and apologized about the banging. Giggling to herself, she wondered if she could do it again and get away with it.

An odd thought came to her as she remembered the pleasure. Each orgasm she'd experienced tonight had been followed by a golden glow and wondered where it had come from. Stephanie also remembered it had felt as if the two men had read her mind through the entire period of lovemaking. The nipple clamps had taken her entirely by surprise, sending her to the verge of orgasm. The Ben Wah balls one of the brothers had inserted into her pussy soon after the clamps on her nipples had been introduced, had been the final push driving her screaming over the edge into one.

She was still imagining the last ride on the dresser, when Mitch came over and scooped her into his arms.

"Oh!" Stephanie groaned aloud. She couldn't help it. She wasn't exactly sore, but her muscles protested the strenuous activity she had been doing.

"Be at ease. We'll make it all better." The rumbled purr sounded in her ear.

Carrying her to the bed, both Mitch and Kristain arranged her so she lay on her side. Kristain climbed in behind her, spooning her, and put his hands between her legs.

"We have a cure we intend to put to good use." Kristain crooned softly.

Kristain made soothing noises in her ear and began to massage her thighs. Mitch lay down in front of her with his head in the juncture of her thighs and laved softly at her nether lips.

Soothed, she barely noticed when a thick pillow was placed between her knees and Kristain asked her for entrance. She gave her agreement on an indrawn breath and he slipped gently into her pussy.

There was an ache there now which had very little to do with pain. In fact, the only discomfort she felt was the agony of unfulfilled desire.

Kristain rocked his way slowly until his condom encased cock was buried hilt deep and touched her core. Mitch had caressingly opened her petals and was using the flat of his tongue to rasp her clit.

It was pure torture. She tried to move her hips in a faster rhythm, but both men grasped her hips and stopped the attempt.

"Please…" she pleaded.

She was trapped in a cocoon of male heat. Kristain's breath was hot and excited on her neck while Mitch's breath teased her thighs. She wriggled as best she could to bring some kind of relief. No one could stand this much sensory stimulation and live.

Yes. She was going to die of pleasure. She was delirious with it and would expire any moment. But what a way to go!

It was the last thought she had as Mitch increased his tempo and Kristain picked up the pace. Every pleasure nerve ending woke up another and another, as the men got serious with their part. She was one big ball of near bursting orgasm and they were doing their level best to keep her there. Neither of the men seemed to want her going over just yet and she almost opened her mouth to beg.

The thought had barely cleared her mind when Mitch tongued her gem a last time and Kristain gave a final lunge. Stephanie dropped off the edge of the peak and fell into orgasmic bliss for what felt like ages.

When the last of the shuddering subsided, the blackness around her eyes cleared and she felt the kisses Kristain laid on her head and cheek. Mitch was gently laving at her bud again, trying to soothe her.

"Pleeaassse, I...a min...ute—" She could barely get the thought out to ask them for a moment. Almost four hours straight of sex wasn't a world record by a long shot, but it was for her. She needed a reprieve and water, and not necessarily in that particular order.

"Ah, little one. We aren't done quite yet, but we sense you need a—refueling break?" Mitch slid up the bed to lie face to face with her.

She kept her eyes closed and nodded. She felt the bed shift in front of her and shivered at the heat loss.

Kristain reached behind him and groped for the covering bunched there. He brought it over himself and tucked it around Stephanie, making a cozy pouch of heat.

Bringing his hand under the covers, he stroked his hand down the side of her closest to him. Loving the feel of her silky skin, he marveled at the thought he could touch her now whenever he wanted to.

She was theirs. No one could take her away. She had consented, had even wanted to beg, for the feel of them inside her. Soon, they would have her in every way possible. Just the thought made his cock rock-hard again.

She stirred at the feel of his lengthening bulge and whimpered slightly.

"Shhh, it is a reaction I have whenever I think of you. Your body grasps mine so tightly and you fit as if made for me. You will have your intermission and then I will bring you yet more pleasure."

On the verge of sleep, Stephanie had felt Kristain's burgeoning shaft growing to its impressive length and wondered if maybe she could go just one more round.

Mitch searched through the refrigerator and grabbed a couple of bottles of water. He opened a package of lunch meat and ate five slices of ham washing it down with one of the bottled waters and looking around for something to carry most of provisions back into the room.

"Hey Stephanie? Where do you keep…"

Opening cabinets as he spoke, he spied what he needed and was reaching for a basket when he felt Stephanie's body clench around Kristain's shaft one more time.

Taking a deep breath and blocking the sensations as best he could, he grabbed the basket hurriedly and returned to the fridge. He grabbed things at random, the last fruit and some jars. He stuffed as much into the basket as he could and what wouldn't fit he clutched against his chest with his free hand.

Padding barefoot back to the bedroom, he found Kristain and Stephanie in the throes of yet another orgasm.

Smiling like a proud papa, he placed the items in his hand next to a few of the catalogue toys and carried the basket to the bed.

Watching as Stephanie came back to herself, he lifted the blanket and climbed under the covers. He placed the basket between himself and Stephanie and began opening a bottle of water.

"Stephanie?" He waited a moment.

"Stephanie?" He breathed gently.

He got a mumbled response and took it as a sign she could hear him.

"I have your water here. Let me lift your head and you can have a drink." He felt tender toward her now rather than sexually stimulated. He wanted to give her everything. He wanted to feed her from his hand, and for her to know that everything she received came from him.

Careful, brother mine, you border on obsession. Come back from the edge. Kristain stayed as still as possible so as not to set Mitch off. Dealing with *Try Nas Ayn*, the unrestrained jealous lust of newly mated males, was difficult in the best of situations. Dealing with it when you were buried in your mate's still pulsing sheath was just asking for a death sentence.

As gently as possible Kristain slowly disengaged from Stephanie, who whimpered in protest. Keeping his mentally linked voice devoid of all emotion, he tried to soothe his brother.

Do not go there Mitch, remember Syne and Asnan?

If Mitch weren't brought back from the edge of *Try Nas Ayn*, he would kill any person who came near his mate. It was a thin line every pair struggled with when first coming together with their mates.

Each of the pair wanted to please the mate, and be the one looked on with favor. If those feelings couldn't be controlled and brought into a balance of shared pleasure, the pair would fight to the death and take their mate with them.

Mitch closed his eyes and took a deep breath, trying to bring his thoughts out of the spiral they'd been in. He knew Kristain spoke the truth. He was going down a road too many of their kind had traveled. He used the exercises drilled into them since long before they could understand why the exercises were needed.

Moments later he found himself with his head in Stephanie's lap as she stroked his hair from his face in a soothing gesture.

He lifted his head slightly and began suckling the nipple hanging so close to his mouth. He couldn't help it. It had been right there for the taking.

Stephanie sucked in a breath. It was an erotic image she was seeing in her head. Her back surrounded by a large male in a protective pose while another large male suckled at her breast.

Would the delights she was feeling go on forever?

As much as she wanted them to, she did her best to disengage the wonderful hot cavern attached to her breast.

"A drink...please." It was all she could manage.

From behind her, Kristain reached out his hand and massaged her breast out of Mitch's mouth. He used his other hand to grab the bottle of water Mitch had been opening when he had slipped into *Try Nas Ayn*.

He put the cold bottle against Mitch's face, making him jerk away from the cold and sit up.

"Ok, I get the point." Mitch mumbled as he brushed at the condensation on his cheek.

Kristain continued to uncap the water bottle and then handed it to Stephanie, who took huge gulping swallows from the bottle.

He looked down at the basket, and then back up to his brother.

"Whachaya got in the basket?" Kristain used his head to point at the basket.

Mitch grinned slyly. "Not really sure as I just happened to be hit by—" he paused dramatically, "lustful thoughts as I was raiding the fridge."

He turned to look at Stephanie, who was breathing heavily from gulping the water, and smiled gently at her.

"Why don't you see if there's something you'd like in there. I'll be more than happy to feed it to you." Lick it off, suck it off, or bite it off of you, Mitch thought as he felt his member throb in agreement.

Taking the last swallow of the water, Stephanie looked for a place to put the empty bottle.

Pulling things from the basket, she vowed to thank her sister for stocking up the fridge. After all, Jan had pointed out, she would need the fuel for this weekend.

How right she had been.

As pleasantly exhausted as Stephanie was from the bed-play, she was starving and could have easily drunk the other five bottles of water in the basket.

Pulling the next item out, Stephanie stopped to take a good look at it. She hadn't remembered putting this on the list she had made for grocery shopping. Looking down at the olives, she wondered if Jan hadn't picked them up by mistake.

Kristain reached over her shoulder from behind her and took the jar out of her hand.

"Ah! Jan remembered!" He looked at Mitch who grinned lasciviously, and then back to the jar of olives. He set about taking the lid off, and taking a couple out of the jar, popped them in his mouth.

Stephanie, who had been looking behind her at Kristain, shuddered. Olives were definitely *not* for her! She went back to looking through the goodies and came upon just what she had been craving.

"Buttered Banana Nut Muffins!" She exclaimed delightedly.

She looked around for a utensil to spread the little pat of butter. Finding none, she decided to use her fingers. She could always clean up later.

She ripped open both packages, broke the muffin in half, and began to slather the butter on one side. She took a heaping bite, closed her eyes in ecstasy, and moaned out loud at the taste of the salty/sweet snack.

"Oh my, that hits the spot."

She opened her eyes and ran them over the heaping pile of food looking for a bottle of water. Her eyes spotted one and made a grab for it. Upon moving it, she also found Mitch's cock fully extended.

Looking up into his eyes, she felt the heat scorch her as his eyes moved from her face to her chest, to the apex of her thighs.

Swallowing the last of the muffin in a hard gulp, she fumbled the lid off the bottle and quaffed as much as she could.

Coming up for air, she coughed as the water went down the wrong way when Kristain's fingers walked over her thigh toward her mons.

Kristain used his other hand to rub her back, trying to help.

"Oh Lawdy!" she gasped. "You two don't ever quit, do you?" She breathed through a few more coughs. Stephanie turned her head and found Mitch beginning to put food back into the basket, clearing the bed.

"Of course not." He soothed. "We would be poor consorts if we did." He finished putting away most of the food and water bottles, but had left a few items out.

Setting the basket on the side of the bed, he moved what was left out, out of the way, then turned to her and grasping her ankles lightly, he gave a gentle tug.

"Lie down, Stephanie." The tone of Mitch's voice dripped hunger.

Kristain took the bottle of water from her hand and set it on the bedside table. He still held the jar of olives, and was planning to put them to good use.

Stephanie wondered at the consort bit, but was immediately distracted when Mitch spread her legs apart and slid her farther down the bed.

She went willingly enough, and was pretty sure what was going to happen. But when he grabbed the jar of peanut butter off the bed and dipped his finger into it, she began to wonder.

A few seconds later, Stephanie felt Mitch smear a coating of peanut butter on her labia and opened her lips to smear it on her clitoris. She shuddered at the cold, and started to protest.

Kristain, who had come to stand beside Mitch, put his finger to his lips and shushed her.

"Trust us. We only want to please."

"I'm new at this. It's...disconcerting. I don't normally follow anyone blindly." Stephanie let a breath out and tried to relax. "You've both already had more of my trust than most. And remember, I'll be wanting my turn with the two of you at my mercy." She eased her muscles as best she could and once again prepared to be inundated with sensuality.

Truth to tell, she really didn't mind being in their hands. So far, she thought it might be just fine being in their capable hands, all the time.

Mitch's eyes twinkled at Stephanie as he climbed on the bed beside her and got comfortable. His hands stroked over Stephanie's breasts and teased her by lightly rolling her nipples back and forth between his fingers, one at a time.

Alternately, one hand would make forays down her stomach to swirl around her belly button causing Stephanie's stomach to jump. Her body was made up of nerve endings and she was following those endings to feel every aching touch.

Stephanie opened her eyes when she felt fingers in her passage. She couldn't remember when she had closed her eyes, but now, she felt herself being stretched and something slightly chilled being inserted.

She propped herself up on her elbows and looked down between her legs. There she saw Kristain taking his hand out of her and dipping it into the olive jar. He brought out an olive between his thumb and forefinger. Bringing it over to her opening, he glanced up to stare into her eyes.

Stephanie felt, more than saw, what he was doing. Her eyes closed to slits as Kristain inserted the olive slowly into her vagina, holding her gaze until she finally lay back to enjoy the stimulation.

Mitch still held her nipple and now bent his head to taste it. He licked it slowly, sucked it into his mouth, rolled it around his tongue, and began to suckle it. Stephanie felt the tug on her breast all the way down to her groin. Between Mitch suckling, and Kristain stuffing her like a Christmas goose, she was beginning to squirm.

Mitch suckled each breast, and then let go to trail his tongue down her chest and past her stomach, stopping just short of her mons. He swirled his tongue and mouth around her waist and into the juncture of her thighs, avoiding her pussy completely. However, he hit a few sensitive spots.

Stephanie felt the bed dip as Kristain, she assumed, made himself more comfortable.

Mitch made his way back up her body and again curved his way around her belly button, stopping to dip his tongue into it on occasion.

Feeling a tongue flatly rasp up her peanut buttered clitoris, she knew Kristain was getting in on the fun.

He didn't stay there long however. A moment later, he began to lap at her opening. Slowly at first, and then as Mitch ran his tongue along his previous path, stopping to taste the peanut butter on her labia, Kristain began to delve into her.

Groaning, she tried to remember if being eaten alive was really a bad thing. Deciding she didn't care, she did her best not to grind her pelvis too hard, and cause one of the men to suffocate.

Stephanie reached her hand out, blindly trying to find Mitch's penis so she could suckle him. When she tried to tug gently to get his attention, he scooted just out of her reach.

Whimpering, she listened as Mitch informed her this was just for her.

Oh no they didn't!

She opened her mouth to speak, but had to wait for a particularly inventive, and searching, tongue to finish its foray before she had her breath back to speak. Panting slightly, she voiced her want.

"Mitch." She gasped. He only grunted.

Close enough to a response.

"I want to...mmm...I want your...cock...in my mouth! Give!" She never realized she could revert to primitive mode in the heat of passion. If she was thinking straight, she might have followed the train of thought more closely. However, she rather enjoyed what was going on instead.

Mitch was quick to oblige.

Scooting around to accommodate Stephanie, he continued to lick the smooth peanut butter off. Slowly, and with great precision, he laved at her until she thought she just may perish from the pleasure.

Stephanie gripped the sheets on the bed and tried to force her hips to still. This was torture. This was what they would make her go through if she was ever tortured for information.

Gawd! She sure hoped they'd torture her some more soon!

Angling her head, she glanced up finding Mitch's cock directly over her mouth. Lifting her head slightly, she manipulated her mouth around his cock to take as much into her mouth as she could.

She reached up and swirled her tongue around his satiny shaft, licking and sucking as his cock slid in and out of her mouth. A drop of salty silk graced her tongue and she reveled in the taste, lapping and suckling in greed at the thought of another taste of Mitch's fluid.

The feel of Kristain's mouth and tongue in her pussy searching for the olives, and Mitch licking at the peanut butter on her clit, and the delicious cock in her mouth, drove her so far over the cliff's edge she continued to scream and twitch in pleasure long after they had stopped their ministrations.

It took her ten minutes to compose herself enough to speak. By then, Mitch had gone to the bathroom to run a hot bath.

Picking her up Kristain carried her into the bathroom. Climbing into the large whirlpool tub, they joined Mitch.

Kristain sat down with Stephanie on his lap and leaned her back against him so she could use him as a cushion.

She tried to lift her hands, but they wouldn't cooperate. She felt soft, wet material under the water touching her leg at her thighs and twitched. This caused the barely banked convulsions to gain strength.

She moaned as another climax, gentler this time, took her.

I think we have applied just a little too much San Na *for now. It's time we let her rest.* Mitch again spoke to his brother in his mind.

I agree, but this will help her muscles to relax. Kristain gave his brother a teasing smile. *I want us to be the only ones who wake up stiff in the morning.*

Both chuckled, rousing Stephanie from her lethargy.

Kristain hushed her and held her close as Mitch cleaned her with as light a touch as possible.

When they had rid her of the peanut butter and cleansed her as best they could, Mitch got out of the tub and took Stephanie from Kristain's hold.

He wrapped them both in a large towel and waited for Kristain to get out of the tub. Kristain stepped from the tub and grabbed a few more towels from the shelf while Mitch carried Stephanie into the bedroom.

Kristain started drying himself as he walked into the bedroom, and watched while Mitch dried her off.

Only periodic moans escaped from Stephanie who had fallen into bed. Mitch climbed in behind her and tucked her into his body. Kristain lay down in front of her so she could spoon him and be completely surrounded by them both.

Chapter 6

Vincent rode beside his brother as both made their way to Ranik. They had been sent by Queen Sara to round up another sack of tax monies that were now two weeks late.

No assignment from the queen was beneath them, but Queen Sara seemed of late to be using most of her strongest warriors to do what she had once termed "chores" meant for underlings. Both brothers had wondered if there was an alternate reason for it, and vowed they'd soon find out for themselves.

Vincent was the first to spot the village. The place looked as if a herd of *dracma* bulls had descended on the village. The buildings were in need of repair, the streets were covered in animal droppings, and any power the village had been able to boast of seemed to be nonexistent. The few people they had seen so far looked as if they were poor beggars who'd not had a meal in days, if not weeks.

Queen Sara had apparently been very busy stripping both land and people of all its assets, and now, the two brothers were here to ask for more.

"Dammit Vincent!" Shan Lin began in a fierce growl. "Do you see what she's done?"

Vincent nodded as he, too, surveyed the surroundings.

"She's going to bring this world to an end, and there's little we can do about it. I have seen it, and I know what will happen if Mitch and Kristain fail to find a bride. We won't surv-" Vincent started to nod in agreement.

Quickly cutting off his words as three men approached the brothers. Shan Lin sat up straighter in the saddle and nodded a greeting to the men who stopped short of his horse.

"What do ya want now, warriors? My body as payment?" One of the men asked in an angry voice.

"No, good fellow. We seek your Elder." Shan Lin spoke formally, his own anger riding him hard.

"You would now seek to deprive our Elder from us too?" A second man asked in a more calm voice than the first.

Shan Lin shook his head.

"No, good fellow. We seek to clear up a misunderstanding. If you'll direct us to your Elder, we'll be about our business." This from Vincent.

The second man now looked toward Vincent before speaking.

"And what business do you have with the Elder?"

Vincent narrowed his eyes at the man though remained relaxed in his saddle.

"That is for the Elder to learn. It is business from the Queen." Shan Lin spoke, still formally.

Shan Lin's rage was banked behind his rigid standard of conduct when dealing with the inhabitants of the Village of Ranik. Both he and Vincent had come through often enough that the villagers recognized the pair, knew the brothers' reputation, and barely tolerated their presence.

Beside him, Vincent still sat relaxed in one of the matching pair of *hookra* saddles they had each been gifted with on their initiation to the Queen's Guards. The animal underneath Vincent was one of the wild horses captured in a ritual the guards went through in training. Both the items were prized possessions of any member in the elite group.

And how the villagers here would dearly love to seize a set and make them their own. More than likely, they would hang them from the most prominent spot in the village as trophies, even if to have the set and not be a guardsman was a crime punishable by death.

Let them try to take my horse and saddle. Vincent spoke into his brother's mind. *At this moment, I'd relish breaking a few dozen bones and would probably suck out the marrow and spit it in their faces.*

Some of Shan Lin's rage eased out of him as he conjured up in his mind the image of Vincent hurling bodies left and right as he drank deep of a boned cup.

Never taking his eyes off the three men in front of him, Shan Lin acknowledged his brother, then began to speak.

"If you three would be so kind as to direct us to your Elder's whereabouts at this time, we can be on our way."

The three men looked between the brothers, then turned and began speaking in low tones to each other.

Waiting for the men to make up their minds, Shan Lin conversed with Vincent through their mind link.

She's done it again. She no more needed us here than she needed us to take the village in the first place. These people have given her everything. There is no more to give!

As he spoke, Vincent also watched the men. If the tension coming off the three was anything to go by, these men were primed for violence. One misspoken word, or a movement made in the wrong direction, could be interpreted as acts of aggression on the brothers' part, and they would have a small blood bath on their hands.

This is only further proof we need to convince Mitch and Kristain of their mother's intentions to bring Aranak to the brink of ruin. You did the correct thing in treating these three as if they were equals rather than ordering them to give you what you desired. These three are ready to snap, and I'd really like to avoid bloodshed if it can be helped.

Shan Lin sent a picture of himself as completely and utterly shocked into his brother's mind, then spoke.

I thought you just said you wanted a fight?

Oh, I do. You know I'm always up for a good brawl anytime, Shan Lin paused a moment. *But I was thinking of taking on the whole village, not literally killing the three in front of us. You know,*

79

something along the lines of a round or two with the locals, then a pint of kritok. *I figured that would take some of the bite out of the dogs here.*

Ah. Mitch nodded his head slightly. *So your anger is directed toward the Queen. Damned understandable. We saw it on the ride here. She's taken everything from them and not given anything in return.*

Exactly.

The three men finished their discussion, then one, the apparent leader, turned back to Shan Lin.

"For now, we'll take you to her. But remember, we're watching every move you make. That bitch queen has taken enough from us, and we'll not give her anything more!"

Both brothers gave a slow nod, then nudged their horses forward to follow the walking men.

Let's see if we can't find a compromise with the Elder here, then you can go to the nearest tavern and see if you can't make a few bets about how many men you can actually take at once. Shan Lin teased Vincent as they ducked to move into a familiar courtyard.

Vincent mentally smacked Shan Lin in the head as he spoke.

I'll take you on any day, brother mine, and we'll see just how good I really am!

That boast said, both brothers dismounted and followed the men inside the hovel they had reached. It was time to bargain.

And it was truly time for the Queen to go.

* * * * *

Stephanie woke to find the phone ringing, a deep baritone singing a bawdy tune, and sound of the shower running. Any of the three was confusing enough, but putting all the sounds together made her sleepy confusion worse.

Waking enough to orient herself, she snaked an arm out of the comforter she was bundled in, and slapped around aimlessly for the phone.

Finding the cradle empty but the phone still ringing, she slapped her hand around in what she thought were wide enough intervals and amazed even herself when her hand smacked on the handset.

She dragged the phone under the blanket and then under the pillow that was currently placed over her head. Speaking into what she hoped was the mouthpiece she managed a croaking grunt.

No answer.

The phone was no longer ringing.

"'Ello?" Was that her voice? It sounded like she was scraping metal over pebbles.

Still no answer.

Mentally shrugging, because it would take too much energy and muscle power to do it physically, she cradled the phone to her chest like a keepsake and fell back to sleep.

No sooner had she dropped into slumber than what she would later swear was the shrieking of the banshees sounded.

It took her three screeches, to figure out it was the phone ringing again.

Being slightly more awake this time, she pushed the on button.

"'Lo?" Silence answered her. She waited for a response, and when none came, spoke again.

"Hello? Is anyone there?" She waited for a reply as she now heard heavy breathing.

"Look, whoever this is, either answer or I'm hanging up." She waited a beat and would have hung up and gone back to sleep if a voice hadn't answered.

"How dare...who do you think...what gives you the right—?" Agitated breathing came through the earpiece before the voice once again spoke. "MINE!"

Stephanie opened her mouth to demand to know who the person was, but a shriek of fury sounded, immediately followed by a disconnect signal.

Stephanie took the phone away from her ear and looked at it as if she would see whom the person had been if she looked hard enough. Finally shaking her head, she hung the phone back in its cradle and gave a moment's thought to who it might have been.

She hadn't recognized the voice, and thought it was probably just a bored teenager with nothing to do on a weekend.

She looked over at the man who still lay in bed beside her and smiled.

Might as well see if I can talk him into a little—as long as I'm up... Her thoughts trailed off as Mitch turned his head toward her.

"Good morning." Mitch rasped as he rolled closer to Stephanie eyeing her with hunger in his look. A look that had everything to do with exactly what she had in mind. The phone call was quickly forgotten.

Chapter 7

By Sunday morning, Stephanie was exhausted. If she expired within the very next hour, she would die a satisfied woman.

Groaning, she rolled out of bed, and examined the pleasant aches and pains acquired from her strenuous workout this weekend.

Even with the deep massages Kristain gave me, I could still go for a hot bath. Though they do say, even if you're stiff and sore, get right back to exercising so the muscles don't stiffen permanently.

The thought made her smile. Getting to her feet, she gave a quick stretch, turning her head to find Kristain asleep in the reclining chair.

She smiled wickedly at the answer she now had for the question her friend Ashley kept asking. Just what purpose the chair had in her room, except decoration? Amazingly, she also found the chair could indeed hold three people who weren't just sitting in it.

Snickering softly so she didn't wake Kristain, she grabbed one of the men's shirts from the floor and slipped into it. She brought a sleeve up to her nose and inhaled deeply. It smelled of a potent male, one who gave off a scent distinct enough to drive her mad. That was all it had taken. The separate smell of each man was unique. Their smell combined when they were together, was enough to make her dizzy with lust.

Sighing in blissful satiation, she strode down the hall toward the kitchen. Along the way, she heard Mitch on her computer playing something which required him to hiss softly and mutter "Die, damn you, die!" and "I did capture the bluebird! What am I supposed to do with the damn thing now?"

Shaking her head as she stepped into the kitchen, she smiled at the thought that a full-grown man still played games like a child.

Making a quick pot of coffee, she poured a cup and took it with her while she went to the front door to get the Sunday paper.

Setting her coffee cup on the hall table, she opened the front door and reached out to the wall where her paper rack hung and grabbed the thick issue. She was just about to go back inside when she spotted a man standing at the end of the hall.

He looked straight at her and doffed his tan Hamburg. This brought her attention to the fact he was also wearing a long tan trench coat. His pants had creases that would put June Cleaver to shame, and the shine on his shoes was probably bright enough to see her reflection.

She nodded her head to return the greeting and the man began to walk down the hall toward her. Suddenly a hand came down on her shoulder and she jumped, shaken.

Turning around, she found Kristain next to her with Mitch just behind him.

Kristain darted his head out the door looking left, then right, and stiffened visibly on seeing a man making his way toward Stephanie's door. Putting himself in front of Stephanie, he pushed her backward toward Mitch.

"Hey!" Stephanie cried out.

Mitch tucked her into his body and wrapped his arms protectively around her. Covered both in front and back, it seemed the two men were trying to shelter her. From what, she hadn't a clue.

Mitch spoke to his brother through their link. *What is the danger, brother?*

Kristain shook his head keeping it turned down the hallway. The man had bolted so quickly after seeing him it was all Kristain could do not to give chase.

Forgive me. Kristain sounded embarrassed. *I lost my head for a moment when I saw yet another man inspecting what is mi...ours.*

Mitch relaxed the hold he had on Stephanie a fraction and waited.

It didn't take long.

Stephanie turned in his arms and thumped Mitch on his chest.

"What was that all about?" She looked at him with a mixture of wariness and suspicion. Turning, she gave Kristain a push, sending him farther out into the hallway.

"And just what is the matter with you?" She gave him the same look she had given his brother.

Kristain shrugged and gave her a look that translated into, 'search me'.

Whirling, she stared into Mitch's eyes and waited.

Mitch gave her a crooked grin and started to caress her arm. She looked down at his hand and back up to him.

"What? Not going to say anything, only try to soothe me?" She waited with barely held impatience.

"No. I would never treat you as if you had no brain." He gave a slight nod of his head. "Kristain seems to have gotten a little green-eyed when he noticed the man in the hall."

Stephanie stood frowning at Mitch. Jealous? Kristain had acted as if she were in mortal danger.

She continued to look at Mitch for a moment longer, and turned as Kristain began easing the door closed. As soon as it was shut and locked, he turned back to Stephanie and met her scrutiny head on. She wanted to ask. No, she needed to ask.

"Is that true?"

Kristain nodded sheepishly.

Stephanie blew out her breath, not realizing she'd been holding it and felt her bristling attitude dissolve. Shaking her head, and more than a tad baffled at the thought that this walking ad for Playgirl was jealous, she walked around Mitch into the living room and set the paper on the coffee table.

She remembered her cup of coffee and grimaced. Oh, leave it. You can get another one when you sort this out. Turning back to confront both men, she found they had come up right behind her.

Stifling a shriek, she closed her eyes.

"Sit." She ordered, pointing to the couch next to them. When she opened her eyes, she found them lounging on the sofa as if they had been posing for a centerfold shot. All that the scene needed to complete the image was for them to be naked.

Swallowing the instant lust climbing up her throat and threatening to choke her, she took a deep breath.

"Listen. I am extremely flattered you would be jealous of another man, baffled, but flattered." She took another breath, "but you don't own me."

There was a heavy silence.

"Did you hear me?" Again, she waited. Surely one of them would speak up and say she was absolutely correct any minute now.

Still, the silence grew, with the men turning to look at each other.

Very good, brother, Mitch said inside of Kristain's mind, his every word dripping with sarcasm. *You seemed to have forced our hand rather soon.*

I want to say I am sorry Mitch, but the truth is, I am not.

Kristain's reply was apologetic, but buried deep within his tone and words, Mitch heard the gladness. *It has been almost three days, and it is unheard of not to tell your wife,* he paused slightly, *that she is your wife.*

Stephanie watched the two of them sitting on the couch staring into each other's eyes. If she didn't know better, she would think they were communicating. And hadn't she thought before that —

Mitch interrupted her train of thought by turning toward her and speaking.

"Stephanie," he looked at her with an intense gaze. "Please," he patted the couch where they were making room for her. "Come sit with us."

Stephanie now eyed them with worry. She wanted to sit with them, but by Mitch's tone of voice, what he had to say sounded — ominous.

"I'll sit right here, thank you." She said as she sat across from them in her love seat.

"What?" She asked warily.

How much do we tell her? Mitch asked Kristain as he tried to bring some order to what he would and wouldn't tell her right now.

Tell her the truth. Kristain admonished. *Out of all the information we have to impart to her, it will be the easiest thing for her to understand at the moment. Look, Mitch, eventually, she has to know everything.* Kristain spoke to his brother and continued to keep eye contact with Stephanie as he went on. *Just tell her she's married to us now, and we are her husbands. The rest can wait.* Mitch heard the implied for now.

Reaching across the coffee table, Mitch and Kristain both took one of her hands, and told her the truth.

"Stephanie."

She looked from one to the other warily. "Yes?"

"Kristain was jealous, because—" Mitch broke off as Kristain jumped in.

" —we are your—"

" —husbands."

They both said in unison.

Stephanie gaped at them, her mind a vast black void. Had they just said—no, she thought. It couldn't have been what they—Married? Husband—?

No. Husbands!

She began to shake. It started in her belly and she made a strange sound. It came out as an *eeep*. The shaking grew until she pulled her hands away, tightened her arms around herself and doubled over.

Mitch and Kristain looked at each other in concern. Getting up together, they went around on either side of Stephanie to kneel at her feet. She shook so bad they both felt the love seat shaking under her.

Mitch reached out to put his arms around her, and Kristain did likewise from the other side.

She is overwhelmed brother, Kristain said seriously.

We will comfort her, then see to her needs. She will not feel so out of control once we… Mitch's voice trailed off as Stephanie raised her head.

After a much needed deep breath, Stephanie came out of her crouch roaring with laughter. Tears streamed down her face as she tried to suck in air.

Both men sat back with expressions of relief, mixed with exasperation.

I somehow get the impression she isn't taking us seriously. The sarcasm was deep in Mitch's voice as he watched their wife laugh uproariously.

It took her a few moments to get herself under control; even then, she still felt stray chuckles struggling to escape.

Kristain opened his mouth to assure her they were indeed men and wife. Joined through the act of consummation. And even now, if they wished it, she could be carrying their children. The condoms had been for her sake, not theirs. It was easy enough to forgo them.

She didn't give him a chance.

Doing her best not to burst into even more laughter, Stephanie tried to grasp what they had just said.

"You...you—" *Yes, deep breath,* she said to herself. "You said...you were my—" She couldn't help it, she laughed as she blurted it out, "...both of you...my...Oh God!...Husbands!"

Every time Stephanie looked at either of the brothers, a fresh spate of laughter would erupt from her causing her to howl anew.

It took a few moments, but when her laughter finally died down to a few chuckles, she looked back and forth between the two and shook her head. Neither looked amused. The closer she looked, the more she noticed neither one was laughing either. They had sat through her howling laughter and said nothing. They hadn't joined in. Come to think of it, they hadn't even tried to deny it.

"I realize you find this—" Kristain looked toward Mitch for help.

"Hilarious?" Mitch made it a question.

Kristain glared at Mitch.

Mitch's eyebrow rose. "Really, dear brother. You must know to attempt that would be impossible."

Kristain glared at him, then back to Stephanie.

"As I was saying. You seem to be under the impression we are joking."

Stephanie watched the two men, eyes wide in wonder, while the two appeared to speak with each other without saying a word.

"Well, you must admit it is a rather comical statement." She smiled gently at him. "I mean come on. How many women have you met who have more than one husband?" She shook her head and let a small chuckle escape. "I don't think I know of a woman who would mind, but I sure know too many men who would be appalled at the idea."

She looked at Mitch. "Do you two do this often?"

He gave her a questioning look.

"You know," she gestured between him and Kristain. "Put on this…this…well, play this practical joke on other women?"

Mitch shook his head.

"No. You are the first woman we have ever chosen as our wife." He looked at Kristain, then turned back to Stephanie and saw a questioning look in her eyes.

"What do you mean by 'chosen', exactly?"

Kristain picked up the conversation. "In our world, it is custom to choose a wife."

She squinted her eyes at Kristain. "Did you just say 'in our world'?"

Kristain nodded. "Yes. In our world."

"But…but…but—" Her mind whirled. What had she gotten into with these two? Her hand flew to her mouth to hold back her gasp. Pulling her hand away just as quickly, she blurted out.

"Are you two—"

She couldn't bring herself to ask. She groaned as she put her head in her hands. It couldn't be. She had—she brought her head up to really look at the two of them. They looked sane enough.

"Are we what?" Came from Mitch.

She turned to him to find a set look on his face.

"What?" Her mind was going in too many directions at one time.

"I asked, are we what?"

Stephanie played the question in her head hoping to bring back the obvious question she had been asking. Finally remembering, she blurted it out so she wouldn't lose her nerve.

"Are either of you on psychiatric medication?"

Kristain tilted his head sideways and looked at her questioningly.

Mitch had no trouble deciphering what she meant. "She wants to know if we're loony. Do we belong in an asylum?"

Kristain frowned, then sighed heavily. He shook his head and turned back to Stephanie. "Really, beloved. We are married." He stroked a hand over her forearm.

She shook her head as he continued.

"Let me tell you the rest." He took her hand in his.

Stephanie gave him a patronizing smile, as if to say, 'Sure buddy, I'll go along with it' and sat back to listen.

"In our world, we choose our wife when we meet her for the first time." He paused thinking a moment. "Well, there are a few exceptions to the rule."

Mitch picked up the conversation. "Sometimes it takes the first encounter to make up a pair's mind. There have been a few who have even waited until the fifth encounter to seal the marriage." He had also begun to stroke her hand. "But those rarely work. They are filled with so much lust the pair end up burning the trio out before they can form any kind of bond."

Stephanie finally realized they were both serious. She tried to take back her hands, but they both held her firmly.

"There are a lucky few," Mitch stared into her eyes as if he was trying to impart pertinent information to her, "a very, lucky, few, who connect and bond," his eyes grew heated, "instantly."

He all but purred the words. She looked from him to Kristain, who seemed to have been infected with the same heat. They both came up off the floor in a fluid motion and began to stroke more than just her arms.

She shook her head. This couldn't be happening. All she had wanted was a new experience. Instead, she seemed to have gotten not only the best sex of her life with two of the most gorgeous men she would ever meet to worship her body, but marriage—with TWO husbands?

It was so much to take in she let it go for the moment and gave in to the heat in their eyes and let them distract her for a few wonderful moments. But as much as she tried, she couldn't seem to get their words out of her head.

She disengaged Mitch's mouth from her breast with more reluctance than she wanted to admit, and brought her hand up to gently push Kristain away from her mouth.

Breathing heavily while her senses clamored for more, more, more, she took a last deep breath and tried to calm her galloping heart.

"You two…aren't…kidding…are you?" She searched both their faces for some sign they weren't serious.

"Suzanne Somers isn't going to jump out at any moment and say 'You're on Candid Camera', is she?" She asked in an unsure voice.

Both men shook their heads.

"No?"

She was beginning to sound as if being married to these, to-die-for, god-like…well, virile males, would be a BAD thing. *Really, Stephanie. You could just go along with it and humor them. What was it going to hurt? It wasn't as if they were here claiming their husbandly rights, or —*

No, she thought as she blushed, *husbandly rights be damned, they'd already had her, and she was rather hoping they would do it again — in excess!*

And soon!

The more they began talking about what their marriage would entail, the more she was beginning to take to the notion of two husbands. They would provide for her, lavish her with love and security. It would be their duty to ensure her happiness, to ensure her continued good health, and guarantee continued satisfaction in their marriage bed.

She grinned broadly at that. Imagine a marriage where it was a man's duty to guarantee the woman orgasmed! Wait until she told Jan! Her sister would definitely pitch a fit then.

The morning continued in a surreal daze, and she was surprised just how seriously the two men took their marriage. They'd been looking for almost twenty years, for a wife who would accept them both.

Stephanie knew they seriously believed what they were telling her, but she was skeptical still. She also wondered if she would have any say in the matter. She finally interrupted their lists of benefits to being married to two men when lunchtime rolled around.

"Look, guys. My head is spinning with the amount of information you've given me to take in. Why don't we stop for lunch?" She looked to both men for their agreement.

"Whatever you wish." Mitch lifted himself off the floor with an easy grace and strolled toward the kitchen.

Kristain got up with him and followed.

Stephanie let her head fall to her chest. It had been hours since she had gone to the door for the paper. She had left her coffee—somewhere, and hadn't gotten anything else.

First things first, she thought.

Her mind might be full of husbands, but her brain was telling her she would deal with it better after a pot or two of coffee. She thought for a moment then decided to add brunch.

✳ ✳ ✳ ✳ ✳

"Well. That took off the edge." Stephanie said as she nibbled on the last of the Chicken Kiev she had made. "Now, if I can get out of this chair, there are a few questions I have, and a few things you gentlemen need to hear."

Looking at the two of them, she almost hated to burst their happy bubbles. But what was a woman to do with two husbands?

Hearing the thought run through her head, the wicked side of her laughed. Okay, so she knew what to do with two husbands. But she had been talking about the practical aspects of it. She calmly began outlining her arguments to Mitch and Kristain.

"First, let me apologize for earlier. I was laughing at you when you were serious. But you both must look at it from my point of view. I met you two days ago, and I don't know anything about your background." She paused as the two men nodded.

"I know there are many women who would be ecstatic at this arrangement. In fact, they'd step over, around, and on me to have the two of you at their beck and call, even without marriage. And speaking of marriage, you do know in California, heck, in most of the United Stated, polygamy is illegal?"

They shook their heads.

"Well, it is." Stephanie stated.

Mitch smiled gently and took her hand, "No, my lovely. We do indeed know about the laws. It's just they do not apply to us." He said gently as he brought her hand to his lips.

Stephanie stared at the top of Mitch's head, then darted a look toward Kristain.

"It is true, *Kasha*. In our world, we do not have this law." He took her other hand and also brought it to his mouth for a kiss.

"In our world, a woman may choose as many husbands as she wishes. As long as all the parties agree and are happy, who is to say this is wrong?"

Stephanie immediately asked. "But what of the men? Do they get to choose as many women as they like?"

"It is entirely up to the people involved." Mitch, while still holding her hand, stroked her shoulder, and went on.

"So long as all involved consent, there is no problem." He turned his head to the side bringing her hand against his face to rub it across his cheek like a cat.

"There is however one exception." Still soothing Stephanie, Mitch continued. "If you are part of the royal family, you are excluded from this law." He looked into her eyes.

"In the royal family, where the line of succession is concerned, twins, if male, may only have one wife; if females, then one husband. This is to ensure any offspring of the union comes from one of the royal family."

Stephanie looked into his eyes and found there was something in the look that said she needed to pay close attention.

"Yes…well…does this mean if I want I will be able to have even more husbands?" Stephanie said in all seriousness.

She felt the tension immediately, even before either of the two men blurted out an authoritarian "NO!" Slightly taken aback at what appeared to be an unquestionable response, she blinked rapidly a few times and tried to gather her composure.

"Um…okay." She swallowed a nervous giggle. "Does the sharp note in your voices mean you won't tolerate another man, or you're from the royal family?"

Both men muttered about not adding more men to their families and avoided actually answering the question.

"Then, on another note, I have some problems with this marriage."

* * * * *

Babbet paced angrily from one end of the sectional couch to the other. The pacing wasn't helping at all to bring her rage under control. She held her arms across her chest and squeezed her arms. She knew she would have bruises in the morning, but frankly, could have cared less. She stopped only long enough to look at Stanley Labowsky and mumble dire threats.

"Don't take it out on me. I'm just the messenger." He sat in his stylish clothing and smoothed his tie for the second time.

He watched as Ms. Carlson paced and muttered to herself and thought this was one of those cases he should have turned down. Even if the amount she'd offered him to watch the twins had been almost half of what he'd made in the last seven months.

She had told him she only wanted him to make sure her boyfriends weren't cheating on her.

Hah! Fat ass lie he had known it was, he had still taken her money and thought it would be a piece of cake. Watching her now with her fist clenched and what looked to be the wrath of Kahn burning her eyes, he knew better.

Stanley had tried his best to convince her that now the men had been found with another woman, it would be her job to confront them. He started to open his mouth. When she turned back toward him, he thought better of it as her eyes drilled holes through him.

"What?"

Well, maybe I'll just wait. "Nothing really." Then he thought, now or never. "No, since you asked. My services seem to be done. I did what you asked, spied on the men, and now that you know—"

He trailed off, as the temperature in the room seemed to drop fifty degrees. She stood in place and seemed to gather herself. Taking a deep breath and closing her eyes, Babbet held her breath for a few moments, and exhaled as if letting go of all emotion. When she opened her eyes, the anger seemed to have left, and she gave him a serene smile.

"Now, Mr. Labowsky." He knew the kind of smile she now wore, and knew to be wary of it.

Gulping hard, he stuttered out his name. "Ca..call me…St-Stan-Stanley."

She continued to smile at him, and her smile grew larger as she walked closer to him. When she was almost standing in his lap, she looked down at him and fluttered her eyelashes a few times.

"Really Mr…Stanley. I think there are all kinds of ways you can still help me." She stopped to give him a smile, one that usually made men sit up and take more notice of her.

Stanley swallowed at the look Ms. Carlson bestowed upon him. He knew if he stayed just one more minute, he'd do whatever she asked.

Babbet held the smile for a few more seconds, and then kicked it up a notch. She watched as the big sap in front of her took her bait, hook, line, and sinker.

"Shall we talk, Stanley?"

And with those fatal words, Labowsky was doomed.

Chapter 8

Stephanie sat in silence and waited for either of the two men to object. When they did nothing but sit quietly, she took a breath and voiced her problems.

"First of all, a woman likes to be asked for her hand in marriage." She watched for clues that either of them was listening. When again they said nothing, she continued.

"There's the little detail I don't even know you two all that well. Like what either of you does for a living. What about your family, your likes, wants, needs? What happens if we disagree? Do I get my way? Does one of you get yours? Can we argue about it?"

She drew a deep breath again and would have continued, but Mitch and Kristain just sat there.

"Look. These are things I need to know. I need some input from the two of you, especially the thing about asking. You can't just arbitrarily announce we're married and expect me to go along with it."

She waited.

She seems to be objecting mostly to the fact neither of us asked, Kristain said to Mitch. *Are any of those questions you'd like to tackle, or would you rather I did?*

Mitch sat back but hung onto Stephanie's hand. I think I'll take most of them. Feel free to interrupt if I leave anything out.

"Where to start?" Mitch mused. "You threw so many questions at us." He thought for a moment, and came to a decision.

"Let me start with a few of the other questions and then we'll get back to the asking one." Mitch leaned back in his chair and let go of Stephanie's hand.

He looked up at the ceiling as if trying to remember.

"Ah yes. What do we do for a living?" He smiled winningly at Stephanie. "We're in the family business and we manage a department in the company. Since you have married us—"

Stephanie started to interrupt him on this point, but he held up his hand to stop her interruption.

"Yes, I know. Our full names are Kristain and Mitchell Anaksup. We come from the Queendom of Aranak. Our favorite color is—what?" Mitch dropped the legs of the chair to the floor abruptly and reached out to grasp Stephanie's arm.

She had gone completely white when she heard the 'Queendom of Aranak'. He frowned as she started to breathe heavily.

"You…again…why…nooo!" Stephanie dropped her head to the table and groaned.

The Queendom of Aranak. Where the hell was that? And just what in hell was she doing even entertaining their delusions? She lifted her head enough to take in the picture of two concerned males and then dropped her head back again, groaning.

They were visions of what she imagined Apollo and Ares looked like in their heyday. Women would drool over them until they died from the wanting. The same women would have fantasies about these two men and put themselves in her place.

Why? Why couldn't they just be close to sane? She sat up and sighed heavily.

"Look. It's one thing to say we're married, two husbands and everything. Hey, I can just write it off as eccentricity. I could probably even go along with it. You two are wonderful men. The sex is fabulous, you both are gorgeous, and hey, I'm available." She paused to argue her point here. "But, you have to hear everything you two have said to me from my side."

She shook her head.

"You were invited for a threesome this weekend, and that's what I got. Thank you for that. But now, I'm supposed to believe all three of us are married, you both are from a place called The Kingdom of Arbneck—"

Kristain interrupted her, "Queendom of Aranak."

"Yes. That Queendom, thank you—what am I saying?" She asked in exasperation.

"The point is, no matter how gorgeous you both are, how good the sex is, shoot, how good it all is, I don't think, no—I know I can't believe either of you are anything but human." She paused briefly.

"Is there any kind of proof—" She trailed off as Mitch stared into her eyes and gave her one of the quickest proofs he could think of.

His eyes became a glowing bright golden color. Shots of light sparked out of them and disappeared like fireworks. He grabbed her hand and placed it on his erection.

"This is what you make me feel. I am aflame with want of you. I want to worship at your altar."

Stephanie watched transfixed as Mitch's eyes continued to spark. She only turned away as she felt a hand grip her shoulder.

Turning she found the same light show going on in Kristain's eyes.

"Have you not noticed what you kindle in us when we climax? This has happened every time, and it pours out of our entire bodies." Kristain said in a sensual voice.

Stephanie stared, gaping. Just how many more surprises were they going to pull out of their magic bag?

"I...I...I thought it was...I thought...I was seeing...stars...because of—" She trailed off while color bloomed rosy in her cheeks.

Kristain and Mitch chuckled huskily as if she had stroked their egos.

"In a way, you were. What you see in our eyes is what you feel in your body when you orgasm." Mitch watched as Stephanie became dumbfounded with what he was imparting to her. He reached out and picked her up. He placed her in his lap and cradled her as if she were fragile.

"Do not fear us, love. Even when the fire burns red in our eyes because of anger we are sworn to protect you above all." Mitch said as he gently stroked her hair.

Stephanie listened to the rumble of Mitch's voice and felt comforted. He seemed to be trying to explain something to her, but she had plenty to deal with as it was.

When she thought she had herself under control, she patted Mitch's arm and started to sit up. Mitch helped her, but when she was upright in his lap, he let her go as Kristain hauled her into his lap.

"Rest assured we will keep you safe in our homeland. You will want for nothing, and you will be adored by all." He kissed the top of her head. "You will rule with an iron fist in a velvet glove. You will be the best sovereign our world has seen yet."

Stephanie wrinkled her forehead as she gave Mitch a confused look.

Rule?

Royalty?

Family Business?

Her mind had finally recovered and she was beginning to connect the dots.

Rule? Rule!

"NO!" She shouted it into Kristain's ear. "I will NOT rule anything!" She heard the hysteria in her voice and took several calming breaths.

"Look! I am not royalty, I'm not even sure we're really married. I haven't even been asked to be married, let alone stood in front of a priest and taken vows." She was rambling. "I haven't signed anything, and we haven't even gotten a blood test. Okay, so you've met my family, Jan, but you still haven't told me anything about yours."

She sputtered out more protests as she thought frantically for a reason she was unfit to rule anything.

"My company!" She shouted again as she realized it would mean leaving her work. "Ha! I can't leave my business." She sat up in Kristain's lap and emphasized her point by poking her finger into Mitch's chest.

"I'm contracted for two films and four commercials in the next seventeen months. I signed contracts in good faith and I don't have a choice."

She smiled smugly. "I can't possibly rule anything, or anyone." She leaned back into Kristain's chest and felt as if she had won the round.

Mitch gave his 'I have you where I want you' grin and his eyes bled back to normal.

"You will, of course, carry out your obligations. We would never dream of giving you a reputation for not honoring contracts." Smiling sweetly, Mitch watched as she relaxed against his brother.

"Your reign won't start for another two years."

Stephanie launched off Kristain as if she had been shot out of a cannon, and gave Mitch a look of incredulity.

"Didn't you hear what I said?" She looked from one brother to the other.

"I am not royal material. I'm a make-up artist. Not to blow my own horn, but I'm a damn good one. I already have a job, I don't need another one!"

She stood her ground and glared at the two to show she meant what she said. Forget the marriage part for now. Her two so-called husbands would learn she couldn't be manipulated into doing something she didn't want to do!

* * * * *

Babbet waited impatiently for the phone to ring while she showered away all evidence of Labowsky's desire. She had done what was needed to ensure he was thoroughly ensconced on her side.

As repulsive as she'd found the act, she still felt a thrill at the fact she had actually manipulated the man into doing what she wanted him to.

She was riding high on a power trip she hadn't used since her first marriage. She had found her husband would do anything, promise her everything, when he was buried between her thighs. And she made sure he always kept those promises.

Babbet thought of what she had asked Labowsky while he labored toward his climax. She had been safely assured if she said the right thing, made the right noises, he would only hear what she asked. He wouldn't notice that although he was striving for a touch of heaven, she was only focused on her pleasure.

The pleasure of his compliance.

No single man had ever brought her to climax. In fact, Mitch and Kristain had been the only ones to ever send her on the ride to Nirvana by cock alone. And it had still taken both of them at the same time.

Remembering it now, her hand slithered between her thighs as she worked herself toward the edge of climax.

She struggled to keep her attention divided between her pleasures and listening for the phone. All it would take was the right words spoken into her ear.

A few moments later the phone rang, causing the ripples to start. She plunged her fingers as deep as they would go. It took her over the edge as she screamed through the orgasm, which rocked her as thoughts of Mitch and Kristain plunging deep went through her mind.

When she could think again, she stepped out of the shower and grasped the handset on the bathroom counter, bringing the phone to her ear.

"Hello." The voice she heard through the earpiece sounded like liquid sex, and it excited her anew. Thinking only of the pleasure that just slammed through her, she began to tease herself again as the caller told her of the success he'd had in his given assignment.

She purred her pleasure out as she thought of the possibilities to come, then laughed at her clever pun.

Chapter 9

Stephanie shivered as she felt Kristain's tongue lave at her clitoris. She was so close to the edge she began to move against his tongue for more friction.

Finally! She shouted, then groaned in sensual abandon as her orgasm burst over her in scorching waves.

Mitch kept up his rhythm of slow thrusts as she rode the orgasm to its farthest reaches.

Both men had made such persuasive points about talking things out later she had barely noticed when the conversation had turned to sex. They had ignited the fire in her to such an all-consuming heat she had given in to them just to extinguish the ache, which had become constant whenever they were near.

Not that she had forgotten about the discussion. Because she hadn't. But a girl had to have her priorities, didn't she?

Well, of course she did. And Stephanie was going to make their final day together last as long as she could. Monday was coming all too soon, and she had to be on a set for—

The thought flew out of her head as Mitch picked that moment to slip out of her.

"Hey! Just where do you think you're going?" She used her elbows to prop herself up on his chest and turned her head back to look at him. She felt his hands slide down her sides and grasp her hips.

"Why, nowhere. But I have this insatiable urge to be buried inside you again—" He trailed off as he wiggled a bit.

Stephanie gasped as she felt his cock at the entrance to her backside.

ari Byrne

"Ummm—" It wasn't that she didn't want to try this, just he needed to know she never had.

"Sssshh. Relax. We'll make this good for you." Kristain said as he eased her back onto Mitch's chest.

"But…I haven't ever—" She wasn't going to be embarrassed about this, she thought. God, please. Not after everything they'd done all weekend.

"And never—with two at a time." She finished in a rush.

Kristain smiled at her gently. "Stephanie, we're not both going to be in the same place at one time."

Stephanie did blush now. But she held up her chin as best she could while she felt Mitch's chest jerk.

"I didn't think you were going to be. I was trying to tell you I hadn't ever tried this. I'm…not…experienced."

She felt the laughter stop at this admission.

Mitch leaned his head into her neck and kissed her neck gently as his arms came around her and held on tightly.

"You don't have to do this if you don't want to." Mitch's voice held a tone that said it wouldn't in anyway make a difference if she preferred not to.

She closed her eyes at the understanding in his voice and when she opened her eyes, Kristain smiled at her with a look she had never seen before in a man's eyes.

Right now, she didn't want to analyze it too closely. She smiled back and sighed deeply.

"No. I want to try this, but I…I'm not really sure…what to do." She would have felt self-conscious if Mitch hadn't given her a final squeeze and enthusiastically reassured her they'd take care of everything this time.

"We'll be gentle. If anything bothers you, we'll stop. There isn't anything you need fear. Ask for it and we'll provide it. Please, " Kristain's voice dropped several octaves as the excitement in his voice came to the fore, "never fear us."

"We would never do anything you don't want us to." Mitch reiterated.

At their reassurances, Stephanie relaxed and let them introduce her to what she had always thought of as a true *ménage à trois*.

Stephanie looked toward the naked brothers as the two went about making a comfortable spot on the living room floor. It surprised Stephanie the men hadn't wanted to do this in bed. She had assumed it would be easier on all if there was a mattress underneath them.

When the brothers looked at her questioningly, Stephanie had shrugged off her assumptions. She knew people could have sex anywhere; she just assumed it would be more comfortable in a bed.

The guys had gone on to explain that, changing positions wouldn't need to be thought about, they could just do it. No falling off the bed or bouncing a mattress off the box springs. This way, they would have plenty of room to fit three bodies.

It was at this time Stephanie had announced to the brothers there happened to be one more tiny detail she would like to ask them to include in their *ménage à trois*. If neither man minded, she wanted to leave the curtains wide open for anyone to see.

It wasn't as if they were on the ground floor or anything, but it still titillated Stephanie to think perhaps, someone actually might see them. The whole point being that Stephanie felt safe, but knew somewhere in the back of her mind, there was always the chance she could be seen.

That thought in and of itself, brought an excitement she couldn't explain even as she told Mitch and Kristain about it. Both of the brothers smiled in understanding.

"We, too, have fantasies. We are here to serve you and will grant you any wish within our powers to give." Kristain extended his hand in invitation, and Stephanie walked over to take it.

"Would you by any chance like to video tape our encounter today?" Kristain asked as Stephanie straddled Mitch's body and stood waiting.

Stephanie knelt down and sat on Mitch's lap, her pussy coming into direct contact with his cock. The feel of it, hot and hard, and ready for action sent a shiver through her. It was silk and satin, as well as hot and deliciously hard. Biting her lip at the feel of Mitch, she looked toward Kristain who began to kneel next to her.

"It might be something I'd like to try." Stephanie's voice sounded breathy as Mitch chose that moment to arch and grind his hips. Stephanie's already wet pussy twitched and pulsed in response and seemed to cry out for her to grasp Mitch's cock and bring it home now!

Stephanie was in full agreement, and rearranged herself for just that. She felt Mitch's hands grasp hold of her hips as she grasped hold of his cock and guided it to meet her eager pussy.

As she sank onto him, Mitch's hips rose to meet her. The sound Stephanie made had Kristain's hand going to his own cock, which leapt at the touch of his palm. The husky moan she emitted was in unison with Mitch's groan and Kristain ached to be inside Stephanie.

Kneeling there, he remembered what he had been about to say just as Stephanie pressed her feet to the floor and rose up off Mitch slightly to adjust herself. Just as she started to sink back onto Mitch, Kristain spoke.

"Just so you know, I did set up a video camera." Stephanie's body shuddered as she continued to sink further back onto Mitch who in return obliged her hungry pussy with a slow thrust. "There was something about the way you have looked toward one of us as the other worked your tight little pussy into an orgasm which made me think you might just enjoy others watching you come."

Damned if the man wasn't right! Stephanie thought. It wasn't something she had ever discussed with anyone, and she wondered just how she had given herself away. It turned her on to know there happened to be more than one person present, that there might be another person who sat and watched as she came.

When Kristain had mentioned the video camera, her heart had started hard, and then began to beat double time. Her pussy contracted around Mitch's shaft and caused him to hold on. It was more than titillation. She hadn't wanted to admit to herself, but merely the thought of another watching her made her pussy drip harder with cream.

The brothers were telling her anything goes in this *ménage à trois,* as long as both of them were there.

Stephanie felt a hand at her butt and found Kristain was massaging her ass. It felt delicious when Mitch ground upward and Kristain grasped onto her ass with two hands.

A lone finger began to ream her asshole and she felt the heated cream they had shown her earlier that they would use to ease their passage into her. Shuddering, as Mitch thrust upward, Kristain began to work his finger further and further inside until Stephanie felt stuffed.

"I...Oh!" Stephanie cried out as she felt Kristain work in another finger and scissor his way inward. She not only felt stuffed now, she felt slightly uncomfortable.

"Easy." She heard Kristain rumble into her ear. Looking down, she watched as Mitch reached out a hand and grasped her clitoris with his thumb and forefinger. The sensations shooting through her became mixed between pleasure and pain. Mitch worked his fingers as both he and Stephanie worked their hips.

Kristain continued to work a third finger into her ass and flex to stretch Stephanie.

Stephanie lay down on top of Mitch, chest to breast as she began thrusting toward Kristain's fingers, then thrusting toward Mitch's cock. Up and down, in and out, until she barely noticed when he pulled his fingers out, and guided the head of his cock into her ass.

Groaning, so very close to coming, Stephanie almost sobbed at the quick loss. Almost immediately, she began to feel the fullness once more as Kristain braced his hand onto her back. The stretching with his fingers into her ass was nothing compared to the large cock he was stuffing into her.

She could feel the two cocks dueling each other as Kristain buried himself deeper and Mitch continued to thrust, holding her hips still with his hands.

Whimpering, she tried to keep her hips still, but the feel of pleasured pain was exquisite!

"Almost there, baby. Ahhh, just like that." Kristain growled into her hair as he continued to thrust.

From the floor, Mitch chimed in. "*Kasha*, you are so hot and tight! I could come right now!" Another moan escaped him.

"NO!" Stephanie shouted. Both men held completely still. "No—" a groan escaped her as her pussy contracted repeatedly around Mitch's cock and her ass around Kristain's. "...you can't...come—"

Her words stopped as both men realized she was close. Feeling exactly what the other was, along with what Stephanie was feeling, they both realized she wanted it to last longer.

In increments, while both soothing and encouraging her in turn, they buried themselves in her tight heat, all the way to the hilts of their cocks.

It didn't take long as Mitch stroked in and Kristain stroked out. All too soon Stephanie could take no more and her orgasm broke over her.

In long vibrating pulses, her pussy contracted and her asshole throbbed in time to the jutting rhythm of the men's cocks as she came, screaming out with short cries of completion.

* * * * *

Stephanie came awake to the smell of food. She took a few minutes to appreciate the fact someone else was cooking, and all she would have to do was clean up.

Looking out of her closed window, she became aware of the fact it was getting later in the day. What would she do when the two men were gone and she reached for one of them to hold onto in the night?

Then she thought about what she had just said and almost smacked herself. Now you listen up woman. You've been sleeping alone for most of your life, and doing just fine. Stop thinking you won't go on doing just that when the two of them leave.

Although, yeah, it sure was nice to wake up with a living blanket on a chilly night, but you didn't have a cloth blanket because Kristain had wrapped himself up in it. It was worth every minute to feel surrounded by those two strong able-bodied males who slept close enough nothing would have a chance of getting between the three of us.

That stopped her.

Nothing getting between them. They were all married. Two husbands. Rule their imaginary Queendom.

Stephanie's thoughts swirled in her head and chased each other. It didn't matter how many things she came up with which were fantastic, she always came back to the imaginary Queendom of Aranak.

Could she really continue seeing them as she had decided she wanted to, even with their eccentricities?

Was the sex so good she —

Well, yes, it was, but —

Think, woman.

Get them to give you a little more than just glowing eyes. You do, after all, work for Hollywood. They could have somehow — she stopped thinking along those lines. She very much wanted to believe they weren't crazy loons. She sincerely wanted these two men to be all they said they were, and they would be able to continue seeing each other.

She just didn't know exactly how they were going to convince her all they'd claimed was real. She got out of bed and walked down the hall. Purposely not getting dressed. She found she actually enjoyed walking around her place with no clothing. It made her feel somehow more feminine. There was also the titillating notion someone might see her.

She entered the living room and found the two of them speaking quietly. She would have liked to stand there without them knowing and watch the two with their heads so close together, probably talking about mundane things. But Mitch looked up and gave her a 'delighted to see you' look.

She returned the smile and walked toward them.

They moved apart and made a small niche for her on the couch. She sat between them and each put an arm around one of her shoulders and around her waist. It felt wonderful. This is how she wanted her life to be from now on.

Mitch and Kristain watched as the contentment fell over Stephanie's face and she snuggled into them.

Do you think she's come to terms with it yet? Kristain asked his brother privately.

I think she's going to struggle with it for a bit, but she seems to enjoy the quiet times as much as the lovemaking. What do you think? Kristain looked into Mitch's eyes and tilted his head to lay his cheek on the top of Stephanie's head.

It feels as if she wants to believe, but can't bring herself to. He sighed softly, and felt the contentment he'd seen on Stephanie's face in his heart. It echoed the sensation his brother was feeling.

Both of them were already in love with her, and she didn't have an inkling of what they'd do to keep her with them.

Kristain felt his brother's deep growl of warning. He unconsciously began soothing Mitch. *Easy.* He continued to look into his brother's eyes and willed him to calm the beast. *She will accept us both soon, and we will be a true* juniane'. Kristain watched his brother's eyes and waited.

If the combination of calming vibrations he was sending his brother and the fact his brother held his beloved didn't ease Mitch soon, all three of them would be doomed to a vicious death.

He willed Stephanie to help him, and was surprised when she moved toward Mitch.

It wasn't that she actually moved out of Kristain's embrace, it was just she was now mostly in Mitch's lap where before she had been between the two of them.

Kristain breathed a sigh of relief as he watched her stroke his brother's thigh and give Mitch tiny squeezes of comfort. His brother's eyes closed slowly and Kristain could actually feel Mitch come back to himself.

He wondered if this was what Mitch had felt when Kristain had seen the man in the hallway earlier.

Yes. And no. He felt Mitch give him a mental squeeze and a gentle thank you. *It felt as if I was losing my link with you. As if our* – Mitch paused to find the right phrase, and could only come up with something close.

It was as if our connection, our bond had grown into hatred, a loathing for each other. I couldn't do anything to bring you back to where you'd gone. You had to make the decision for yourself. You had to want all of us more than you wanted only Stephanie and Kristain. Remember, in our world if one twin rejects the other, they both die.

Kristain gave his brother a mental nod.

Even though we'd passed this stage, and knew everything about each other, it was as if the acceptance of each other we'd gained over the years meant nothing, and couldn't hold us to each other. In a sense, you were severing our link. Mitch closed his eyes and gave another tiny sigh.

Just now, when you talked of her accepting us, Mitch looked down at Stephanie and gave her a kiss on her forehead, praying they all accepted this bond. *I wanted her only to accept me.*

He kept his head lowered for a moment, and then looked back at his brother and tried his best to explain. *There was absolutely no hesitation or thought, to what it would have done to you, or us. If it had gone on, I would have severed our link, damn the consequences.*

You and I were tied together from birth. Mitch gave his brother a feeling of shared memories and love, then continued. I can only say all that I am—All that we are—

Mitch shook his head sadly, hurting inside for what he must confess.

There will come a point in this relationship where neither of us will have a choice of how we bond.

He looked back down at Stephanie and felt the jolt of pure love, pure power, flow through them all. The feeling was incomparable. He'd never before felt anything close to it. Not the love of his brother, the brother who shared ninety-nine percent of his life with him. Not the love of any family member.

The only feeling that came anywhere close to it was their shared orgasms.

Mitch looked up at his brother and found Kristain staring hungrily at Stephanie. One side of him wanted to hold Stephanie as far from his brother as possible, while the other side demanded he share.

There will come a time when she is the only choice we have, and we must pray she does not reject us. She is the one who will decide our fate. Mitch stated as he watched Kristain.

Kristain felt the horror his brother was feeling, and remembered the same sense of terror go through himself when he'd seen the man in the hall earlier.

Shuddering simultaneously, Mitch pulled Stephanie into his embrace a little more, and she snuggled up to him at the same time she held her hand out to Kristain.

Knowing there wasn't a chance in hell of ignoring what she was to him, and would be the same with his brother, Kristain scooted closer to Mitch and Stephanie and wrapped himself in their embrace.

He found himself reaching mentally for both his brother and Stephanie, and when he felt the thin threads connect, he relaxed and let the uncertainty go.

For now at least.

Chapter 10

There comes a time in every woman's life where she made decisions based solely on her urges. This was one of them.

She had told herself she would not give in to the pull of the two males who had wrapped themselves around her as if she were their lifeline in this world. Laughing to herself at her unintended pun, Stephanie lightly patted the body part nearest her hand and then had every intention of getting up to end the weekend.

She wanted to tell both Mitch and Kristain she'd had the most sensuous, relaxing, intense, and wonderful weekend in her life, and would either of them like to do this again sometime?

It's what she had planned on doing anyway.

What actually happened when she finished patting the body part, Kristain's she thought, was the beginning of the hottest sex of the entire weekend. She climaxed so many times that when she had gotten up to stretch, she'd had an orgasm.

She sat now in the warmth of the tub surrounded by soothing oils and felt her vagina pulse still. She laid her head back and tried to relax her muscles. Every other muscle almost cooked noodle limp, but her sex was having none of it.

Two men lavishing attention on every part of her body for the better part of a day and night wore a woman out. By the time Mitch and Kristain had let her rest for a time, she thought she had easily broken some record for the most orgasms ever in one steamy bout of sex.

Her throat was raw from the screams issuing out of her throat every few minutes as the two men drove their cocks faster and higher into her. They were insatiable and had infected her with their drive to give her pleasure.

The massages to her body after orgasming only served to excite her more. The men encouraged her body to take control over her mind and live for only the moment. They played her body like a fine instrument making the tension in her stimulated body sing out in completion only to turn around and start again.

It was as if the men had trained her pussy to pulse on command. All she had to do was think about either one of them, and she was instantly drenched in her own liquid. And God forbid she thought of them both at the same time.

She had done it the one time, and...aahhh.

She panted as she shook with yet more tremors.

A knock sounded on the bathroom door and Stephanie shivered. She knew at least one of the boys was on the other side of the door, if not—

She moaned again loud enough to have the door opening and Kristain poking his head in the door.

"Are you all right?" He asked so attentively she wondered if he hadn't been waiting at the door for an excuse to come in.

"Umm...yes...I—" She could see the smile start to bloom on his face and groaned out loud in what she prayed sounded more like exasperation than sensuality.

She should have known better when he climbed into the tub with her.

"I have something which will make it all better." Kristain crooned to her as he lifted her onto his lap.

She felt the rigid erection against her body and purred at him.

"Oh. You like this, do you?" Kristain asked with a wicked smile on his face.

He reached down behind her and slid his hand along her cleft. He massaged his hands on her buttocks while he kissed his way up her neck.

Stephanie was positive she could take no more. She throbbed so badly she wanted to beg him to sink himself deeply into her, but was certain she wouldn't be able to walk the next day.

Kristain continued his assault on her body, and when he pushed Stephanie close to the edge of orgasm, he entered her mind.

My love. He whispered as gently as he could and sent assurances of love flooding through her body.

I will do anything for you. He paused to move his hand to her breast and felt her at the edge of his lust.

It was happening. Just as both he and Mitch had been told. The connection strengthened with every sexual encounter between them and their chosen.

Stephanie was almost so far gone she would have missed the voice if another pair of hands hadn't joined in the carnal pleasure she was riding.

Wave after wave slammed into her and she cried out in frustration as she tried to climb them.

Kristain was deliberately keeping himself apart from her.

If she had been in her right mind, she would have understood he held back for her sake, not his. But she wasn't in her right mind. She was a woman being denied sexual release, when for the last two days she had been given all she could take.

Stephanie took matters into her own hand, literally grasping Kristain's impressive cock and moving herself over it. She felt as if she could scale towering walls to get him inside of her. She was invincible, and nothing would stop her from having him.

He was hers.

She sank onto him and proceeded to take him on the ride of his life. Somewhere in her mind she knew she had never done anything like this, and didn't have the faintest idea where it came from.

All she knew was she was claiming what belonged to her.

Kristain rode his release for what felt like an eternity.

It was over too soon for him.

Stephanie had taken everything he could give her, and had given it back. He waited for his cock to stop throbbing, and finally realized it never would as long as she was alive.

He opened his eyes but couldn't remember closing them.

Looking up into her face, he became aware of the fact Stephanie had gone into *Ty Na Ran*.

It was the act of claiming the mate, but he'd never seen it, only heard stories. He also became aware of the fact Mitch had joined them in the tub. He looked past Stephanie's shoulders at his beloved brother and knew this was what Mitch had been alluding to earlier.

He also wondered how long Mitch had been there. He tried to open his link with Mitch, but found Stephanie blocked it now.

Joy and elation ran through him as he realized she had accepted him.

He wanted to bathe himself in her warmth and suddenly noticed she had lifted herself off of him. She turned her back on him completely and he knew desolation.

It lasted only for a moment, but it was a bottomless pit of despair he never wanted to visit again.

In the time she had turned from him, she had already mounted Mitch.

Kristain suddenly felt what Stephanie must have felt with him.

He felt her sink onto Mitch's shaft, felt the walls of her passage contract as she slowly, oh so slowly, began to ride Mitch. It was more than he'd ever dreamed of, and yet still less than he'd expected.

The last thought didn't last long as Stephanie increased her pace.

Kristain felt when she was on the verge of orgasm, then he felt the frustration as she backed off from the edge. He wanted to go to her and help. Give her anything she needed. Be anything she needed.

He started to move closer and she turned her head and actually growled like an *averon*. Like a tigress, she bared her teeth, snapped at him as if she would do him bodily harm, and he felt as if she had crushed his heart.

She turned once more from him yet felt a soothing kind of heat enter into his soul. Stephanie, however, physically ignored him.

All her energy was for Mitch.

Stephanie rode Mitch as if she would never have him inside of her again. She ground her pelvis into him and prayed it would not be the last time.

I can only hold on for so long, she thought, then I'm going to go over whether I want to or not.

But she knew, somewhere in the deepest part of herself she had to hold on.

This…this—

Stephanie didn't know what to call it. She knew it wasn't any lovemaking she had ever heard of, and she wanted to be scared.

But there was no room in her right now for fear.

Whatever was happening between her and the brothers had taken on a life of its own. She was on this runaway train until it ran out of steam, or crashed.

She also knew with an instinct that came from an unknown source if they did crash, they'd all go down in flames. There would be no second chance. All three would die, or wish they had.

Things flew through Stephanie's mind as she continued to drive herself onto Mitch's swollen shaft, not giving any thought to her own comfort. Pictures flashed by which she thought she should know but she couldn't hang on to them. They flitted through her thoughts as she pumped the last bit of fluid from his cock and abruptly stood up.

Mitch watched as Stephanie climbed off him and out of the tub.

This was what his father had so desperately tried to explain to both him and Kristain. Mitch had scoffed, and Kristain had laughed through most of the telling.

To think, all that his father had said was true. He had felt Stephanie bite down through skin to find the blood flowing through his veins just as she had done with Kristain. That minuscule amount of blood coupled with the sperm from both his and Kristain's repeated orgasms were what actually allowed Stephanie to be able to hear the thoughts of others.

Mitch tried desperately to reach Kristain mentally, only to find a barrier where his brother's mind had always been. It also seemed to allow her to break the connection between himself and Kristain. He could only now pray she reconnected his mind to his brother through herself. It also made him wish he had paid closer attention to his father when he'd been explaining the ritual.

He looked at Kristain and opened his mouth to speak, when suddenly Stephanie turned to him, bent in front of his face and gave a growling hiss. Mitch's whole body reacted as if she had gutted him. He bent at the waist, his arms going around his middle as if to protect himself.

When Mitch could finally see through the pain he'd been in, he found Stephanie with Kristain's throat between her teeth. He watched with his heart in his mouth as she alternated between biting his brother's throat and lapping at the tiny amounts of blood welling up to the surface.

Mitch felt envy and heartsick. He wanted to be the one she did that to. He craved to be the one she did it to. He started to rise in the water, barely noticing how cold it had become, and found himself facing a bloody mouthed *averon*.

She was splendid in all her glory and he was awed by what he saw. His brother lay with his head tilted, almost completely out of the tub, with blood smeared from one side of his neck to the other.

Stephanie now completely ignored Kristain and—prowled the short distance toward him as if he would scramble to get away at any moment.

He had absolutely no desire to move.

When Mitch finally realized he was connected to her mind, he lay as passively as he could and actually bared his throat. He found he still couldn't feel his brother, but he could feel Stephanie. And at this moment, *she* was all that mattered.

Stephanie watched what she did to Kristain and Mitch from somewhere trapped inside her. She should have been appalled at the things she'd done. But at this moment, all that mattered was the ritual, and the release.

She didn't know how she knew, only that it was now completely vital to the survival of all three of them.

If she stopped now, they would wither and die, fighting amongst themselves with no trust. No love, passion, reason, or sense. Only hatred, accusations, lies, and death. She had no choice.

They belonged to her, and she would kill them herself before she let another touch them.

Chapter 11

Stephanie awoke in her room, by herself, with no knowledge of how she came to be there. She felt strange, and she felt — horny.

With that one thought, it all came rushing back to her in a flood.

Rolling off the bed, she shot to her feet, and raced to the bathroom where she violently vomited. Stephanie didn't know how long she had been crouched there when she felt hands on her head and body. Two hands held her head while another pair stroked her back and shoulders.

She continued to vomit, but it was only dry heaves. When her stomach finally stopped spasming, she tried to sit back and would have slumped to the floor if not for the hands still holding her.

Sprawled on whatever warm, hard surface was behind her, she knew as soon as she thought that the surface was Mitch.

She tried to lift her head and found it hurt too badly. A cloth was held in front of her and she reached up to grasp it. Finding even that much beyond her, she let her hand sink back wanting to cry.

No, little one, do not weep. It is our turn to do all the work.

Stephanie would have bolted straight up in Mitch's embrace if she had found the strength. Instead, she turned her head slowly to the side and found Kristain attempting to wipe her mouth and nose. She felt too embarrassed to have another do for her as if she were an infant, so she reached deep inside herself and found her reserve.

She thought of Mitch letting go of her, and he did. His arms still encircled her, but he let go instantly.

Stephanie thought of the cloth Kristain held, and when she reached up to grab it, he put it into her hand.

Struggling with exhausted muscles, she managed to wipe her mouth, nose, and chin, and wished she had the strength to get up to rinse her mouth.

A cup with mouthwash appeared in front of her along with a strong hand wrapped around it. A thought was in her head to sip some, rinse her mouth and he would help her lean up to spit it in the toilet.

She did this all without much thought, and was amazed after she had done it.

The three of them were somehow communicating without speech.

It was the last thought she had.

Stephanie woke to a world of darkness and found herself once again with two warm, male bodies wrapped around her. The three of them had become one as they slept. She was more than content, she was peaceful, loved, and she knew it was a love that would never end.

Not even in death.

Stephanie awoke next to murmuring. Mitch was holding a quiet conversation with someone who wasn't there.

She is handling it with amazing aplomb. She wasn't born to it, but she acts as if reading minds, hearing thoughts, was no more than the norm.

There was a small pause and Stephanie climbed from the bed. She padded to the bathroom to shower and wondered just who Mitch was singing her praises to. Climbing into the shower, she continued to listen to Mitch's side, and smiled when she felt Mitch stroke her mind.

It was such a new sensation, and one of such unexpected pleasure. Stephanie closed her eyes and a moan escaped her.

With a thought, she found Kristain. He was in the kitchen making a dish she'd never heard of before, something with steak, cilantro, fish oil, green and yellow onion, cucumbers and limes. It sounded wonderful.

Wondering just how the two men had survived all those years living in each other's thoughts, she probed their minds for a way to cut off the link so she didn't have to think, period.

As soon as she thought it, her thoughts became her own again. It felt strange and disorienting. She panicked. Her eyes flew open and she frantically thought of Mitch and Kristain.

The door slammed against the wall so hard Stephanie knew she would need to re-plaster the hole the knob had left. Turning her head at the sound, she watched and listened as both men tried to get through the door at the same time.

The width of both their shoulders together in the doorway was almost twice the size of the doorway. They finally managed to force their way inside and come up to the shower.

Each climbed in still fully clothed to surround her, and wrap her…okay, squashed her between them.

Waves of comfort seeped out from their beings and bathed Stephanie. She wanted to soak in the comfort of the two men, and immediately sought to comfort them.

I'm so sorry. I was just trying to get a moment of time to myself. It was getting overwhelming. She wanted to soothe them as much as they were soothing her.

And you were just bragging about how well I was doing. Stephanie snuggled herself into the two of them and basked for a moment. Her eyes closed in blissfulness as she felt the love coming from the two.

Just as suddenly, her eyes opened and she looked toward Mitch.

Whom were you talking to?

Mitch opened his eyes and looked directly into her midnight blue eyes and almost drowned. It took him a second to let the question sink in.

Giving his head a slight shake, he wondered if she would believe him. *I was speaking with the present Queen.*

"Present Queen. Right." Stephanie had just gotten her emotions under control from one surprise, only to have Mitch thrust another on her.

If she were in any condition to take inventory of what had gone on these last few days, it would read like a list of fiction.

1. Had *Ménage à Trois*.
2. Had the most delicious orgasms of her life.
3. Found out exactly how to use those adult toys she had only read about in magazines.
4. Gotten married.
5. Found out she had married not one, but TWO husbands who would grant her every wish.
6. Found out her two husbands were somehow connected to a monarchy.
7. Woken to find one actually speaking to a Queen.

Anything else she could think of?

She looked between her two husbands and started to shake again. Now, not only did she need to find out how to close off her two husbands, apparently she needed to learn how to keep others out as well.

Kristain looked to his brother as they each tightened their grip on Stephanie and said, *You know we'll eventually have to explain everything to her.*

Mitch nodded absently as he listened to the other voice in his head. *And here you told me she was adapting remarkably well. Do I take it this is no longer true? Have my sons sought wedded bliss in the last place possible only to find there are none who can cope?*

Mitch grimaced as he listened to his mother's snide comments.

How he'd ever thought she would accept the fact they had found her replacement was beyond him.

Kristain was normally the one who remained naive while still being able to see through to people's true hearts. Mitch was the cynical one who prophesied doom and death.

But on this, Mitch had been the one who was sure their mother would come around and Kristain had just shaken his head. After all, Sara knew she would die if she tried to hold on to power after they had established a new Queen.

It had been this that had prompted their mother to contact Mitch in the first place.

He had told her they would wait a little bit before coming home, time enough for her to finish what needed doing, and end her reign in a way befitting a queen of the Queendom of Aranak.

She had laughed uproariously and asked if he thought she would actually give up her throne to one not of their race, let alone not of their world.

The argument had been fierce and if it hadn't been for Stephanie suddenly trying to sever their link, he would have said something to his mother that he would never forgive himself for.

His mother continued to rant at him until he stopped her from coming into his mind. Something that he'd had to learn early, or go insane.

He brought his thoughts back to Stephanie and Kristain and felt the panic flying through his wife.

Be at ease, little one. Mitch said as he stroked her hair and tried his best to send calming thoughts. *It is not what it seems. You will be wonderful.*

Kristain felt the stirring in both Mitch and himself. It was said a trio was rarely like this. The want of the spouses for each other normally leveled off after the initial joining. But for him, as well as Mitch, their feelings seemed to have intensified.

He felt the stirrings grow stronger as his body reacted to the presence of his wife.

He looked up to see Mitch's eyes start to glow slightly and knew he wasn't mistaken.

Stephanie felt the stirrings in both her mind and her husbands' bodies.

She felt hysterical laughter grow inside her and quickly forced it down. She made a deal with herself that after they finished 'soothing' her, she would tie them down and make them understand her fears.

With that thought firmly planted on her to do list, she let go of everything but the hunger growing ever stronger inside her.

* * * * *

Babbet knew exactly when Labowsky had decided he wanted more. It was after she had dropped to her knees and found he was just as hot for her as she was for Mitch and Kristain.

While she had her mouth full, Labowsky did his best to explain what he had done. It came out in starts and stutters, but out it came.

She waited until he had almost told it all, then went in for the kill.

"Now Mr. Labowsky…Stanley," she had to lick the underside just a bit…more. Just the thought of doing this to Mitch and Kristain made her push further.

Before she quite knew it, it was over and instead of her satisfaction, Stanley Labowsky was the one with the wide smile on his lips.

When Stanley could think and breathe normally again, he gathered his thoughts and looked at the woman kneeling at his feet.

From this vantage point, she looked like any other woman who had been in this position, and nothing special.

He wondered just when he'd sunk to taking advantage of his clients. He would have apologized and left if she had just kept her mouth shut.

Looking up at Labowsky from the floor, Babbet glared daggers.

How she had come this low in life, she could only attribute to her obsession with two men. The things the three of them had done —

She was interrupted by her own thoughts, when she realized she was thinking out loud.

"It figures he was a man who couldn't last." Even mumbled, she saw the moment he heard, and did her best to backpedal.

Standing, she reached her hand out to his shoulder and stroked it.

"Well, this leaves all the more time to do it again. And again." She gave him what she thought of as her 'you can't resist me' look and stepped around to the other side of him.

"It all sounds as if things are starting to fall into place. Now, for the next phase —"

And while she spoke, she came back around to his front and used her hand to gratifying splendor.

And he let her.

Little did she know he wasn't so far gone to see her for what she really was. And it would be her downfall.

Chapter 12

Stephanie dried herself as she listened to the boys rustle around in the bedroom. She thought she would attempt to have a lucid conversation with them, but they were making it harder to do with each passing moment.

She swiped at her hair with a brush, then grabbed up the lotion to start smoothing some on.

Mitch came back into the bathroom.

"Allow me." He stated as he tried to take the bottle from her.

She hung on to the bottle as she tried to explain.

"Look Mitch, I think this time I'll just do it myself. It seems every time you, your brother, or both of you put your hands on me, we end up tangled together." She smoothed the lotion down her leg, but kept facing him and the door. "Not that it's a bad thing or anything, it's just—"

Stephanie made a thought, and Kristain appeared.

"Ah, there you are. And no, you can't help either." She made a gesture toward the vanity, "Have a seat. It's time we three had another talk."

Kristain sat and looked at Mitch, who only shrugged his shoulders.

"As I understand it," Stephanie began and reached out to grab her clothing, "you can both read my mind. I know this, because I can now read yours." Even as she continued to speak, she pulled on her jeans and shirt.

Kristain and Mitch both nodded and waited for her to continue.

"Right. And apparently, since I can read every thought in your head, you've already read all of mine." She paused and waited for their agreement.

When it wasn't forthcoming, and there were only denials coming from both of the men, she cocked her head and concentrated.

Both men barely winced as she rifled through their minds.

When she was done and had stopped the direct contact, they both felt a relief more acutely than they had ever before. She was growing in power by leaps and bounds. Their mother had never been anywhere near this strong.

They both would have been apprehensive, but they knew in their hearts Stephanie would only use this gift for the good of the Queendom.

Stephanie took a deep breath and let it out slowly.

"Okay. So maybe you don't know." She looked at both of them and gave a decisive nod of her head. "Here's what I need to tell you.

She sat down on the toilet seat lid and closed her eyes for a moment.

"If you could read my mind when you first got here, you'll remember I was hesitant, even if I was extremely willing." Both men nodded. "Well, I had this apprehension because of a man I used to date."

Swallowing the remembered pain of that one night of her life, she went on. Her voice was low as she told them of the night in which Robert Williams tried to beat her to death.

She wanted it clear he hadn't been able to, as she had fought back with all she was and every bit of strength she had. She had been able to use a few of the moves she'd learned when she and Jan had taken police given self-defense classes and had managed to get away.

The memory still held enough power to bring out the horror of what would have happened had she not been taught to take care of herself. Thank God for her sister's insistence about those classes!

But she had learned later Robert had actually put a woman in the hospital, and the woman's sister had ended up killing him.

"I'm glad I got away, but I now wish I had gone to the police about what happened. If I had, I would have been able to press charges, and the woman he put into the hospital might not have had to go through her trauma." She stared at the floor, not really seeing it. When she let the thought go, she lifted her head and stared both of the brothers in the eye.

"I'm ninety-nine percent positive my sister wouldn't hook me up with…with—" She couldn't think of any thing to call a man of Robert's kind, and Kristain spoke for her.

"A *wajane.*" He sent the translation to her as he spoke the word.

Stephanie smiled. "Yes, that word would be what I'm looking for. A bad man." She tried to give them humor with the telling, but when she saw their faces, she knew it was a good thing Robert was dead.

Mitch kept his anger checked even while he tried to keep it from Stephanie. He knew these things happened, even in the lands of Aranak, but he wondered why a man would feel the need to so dominate a woman that he used physical violence to ensure his power.

He shook his head and continued to listen.

Stephanie sent soothing thoughts to him this time, and it eased the tension in his shoulders visibly.

She preened under the gentle feelings of pride she felt coming from Kristain, whom she had managed to comfort without touching.

Kristain knew it had taken him and his twin no time at all to comfort each other, but it had taken years for them to learn to comfort others. Stephanie had managed to do it in a scarce few days.

Smiling at Kristain's thought, Stephanie continued.

"I only wanted to tell you this because when Robert started to change, the first thing he did was to use my self doubts against me."

She shook her head at the things the man had said to her, wondering how she could have, even for one moment, believed anything he had said.

She brought her gaze between the two men and finished her thoughts.

"Since you've told me I would be a Queen, and I'm still not saying I believe you, the doubts Robert planted in my head have begun to creep back in." She looked to both men now, "And before you think I need to hear what he told me was a load of crap, I already know it. But it doesn't stop the doubts from creeping in."

Both men waited for her to continue. When she remained silent, they both began to assure her she would be fine.

"I may never be fine with becoming royalty, but if it's what has been destined for me, I'll do it to the best of my ability."

And Stephanie knew it would be the end of the denial she still had lingering.

Kristain and Mitch got up when she did and followed her out of the bathroom and into her living room.

She went to the side of the couch and slipped on her sandals.

Turning to find the brothers, she smiled and asked if they wanted to go out.

"I'm feeling a bit hemmed in. We haven't set foot out of the apartment for the past—" She stopped and tried to remember how long ago it had been. "Well, for a while now. I was wondering if you'd like to take in a movie I have tickets for. I can use them whenever I like. And tonight, I want to take you both out and treat you for a change."

These men must be God's gift to her for some major kindness she had done in this life, but she couldn't think of one good enough to warrant them.

"You don't need to entertain us. Do things for us." Kristain said.

Mitch followed quickly, "It is we who will do for you."

Stephanie raised her eyebrows at the comments. "Well, I want to do this for you. So if you need to freshen up…" Her voice trailed off as the look in both of their eyes turned to one of unanticipated pleasure.

As Kristain went to the bedroom mumbling something about changing, Mitch asked Stephanie what movie they could see.

"Anything you guys want. I'll watch whatever you guys want to see."

Mitch reached out to her and pulled her into his arms. He bent her over his arm and kissed her until she couldn't think straight. When he let her up, he managed to steady her before he followed Kristain to change.

Stephanie managed to get her wits back and vowed if this was the response to a movie, she couldn't wait to find out what they would do when she showed them Disneyland!

* * * * *

Stanley stared through the viewfinder of his video camera at the trio crossing the parking lot of the theater. This, more than any other evidence, would be the icing on the cake as proof indeed the three were an item.

You could see by the way the two men moved on either side of the woman and the attention they gave to anything coming toward her. The two men seemed to act more like bodyguards rather than her dates.

They had both been extremely attentive to her while they had all been at the theater.

Who would have thought they would go see a Star Wars movie. She didn't look the type to sit through anything but a romance. Just went to show you could never judge a book by its cover.

She might have bought the tickets, or rather had passes for the movies, but it was the men who had waited on the woman. There had been enough food between the three of them to feed ten people. He'd seen they had one of each item, except the popcorn, they'd each held a bag of their own. He knew, because he had gotten in line behind them, and sat four rows back.

The men hadn't touched any of the food until the lady had, and all through the movie, they had both repeatedly offered things to her. They seemed to wait on her hand and foot.

Never would he do all for a woman. Women were put on this earth to serve, and nothing more.

Just like the fancy Babbet Carlson.

He adjusted his growing hard-on as he thought about just what the lovely Ms. Carlson had done for him on her hands and knees. She must have taken lessons from the Whore of Babylon.

He put those thoughts aside before he needed to take certain matters into his own hands. Right now, he needed to concentrate on the woman in front of him, and he could think about what he was going to do to Babbet later.

He watched as they got into their car. When they drove off, he followed. See, he knew it would easy. All he had to do was find her alone. And he would.

After all, exactly how long could two men stay glued to one woman?

Chapter 13
One week later

Ok, sure it was nice to have two husbands. What girl wouldn't want two husbands? I mean they were doing everything for her. Shoot, they were doing things for her she didn't even know she wanted done!

Things were absolutely great, right?

Even as she thought it, she remembered too late they could hear her every thought.

She waited for the inevitable cry of foul, and when it wasn't immediate in coming, she frowned and turned to go looking for the men who usually came running at even her slightest wish.

She found Mitch back at her computer, where he was steadily killing off everything that moved across the screen. When she entered, he looked up, pausing the game, and sent her a casual brush with his mind.

"Sorry. Didn't mean to interrupt, but I had wondered when you didn't hear what I said. I…ummm—" Stephanie stopped right where she was. If he hadn't heard her, no use letting on she had wanted something.

"Oh, you must have found your off button." Mitch seemed to get very excited by this and Stephanie had to protest.

"No, I hate to be so crude, but my button seems to be in the permanent on position!"

Mitch paused a moment, then suddenly threw back his head and roared with laughter.

Stephanie played back what she had just said and turned bright red. She tried to stammer out a denial, but let it go when Mitch seemed unable to stop laughing.

Smiling at her own expense, she admitted it was kind of funny.

"Fine. So you were referring to the off switch of the open minds. I admit, I guess I've found it. It wasn't too hard. Do you want to know how I found out?"

Mitch managed to stop laughing, with only a few chuckles escaping, and motioned with his hand for her to explain.

"Well, I was thinking I wanted my thoughts to myself, which was what I had been doing earlier when I cut you two off the first time, and suddenly, they were."

Mitch wiped at his tears and nodded his head.

"Sorry. I'm glad you have more control of it. I would hate for you to feel as if Kristain and I were intruding." He came forward to take her hand and brought it to his lips.

"But I am equally glad your 'button' is always 'on'." He gave a slight chuckle while he turned her around and tucked her into his front.

He nibbled on her neck and had her bending it so he could access more.

"I have the perfect way to celebrate your find." He ran his tongue over where he had nibbled as if to soothe the skin.

Stephanie shuddered and found she wasn't averse to celebrating with him.

"I could of course buy you a lovely gift of gold for learning something in a few days it took me a few years to learn." He interspersed his words with more tiny bites over the back of her neck.

"Or…" He continued to place nibbles down her shoulder toward her breast. "…I could give you a gift of diamonds…" He retraced his path back to her neck.

"Or I could just…" He trailed off as Stephanie rubbed her backside into the large bulge in his pants.

"Or you could just give me…" This time Stephanie brought her hand in between them and grasped his rapidly growing desire, "…this."

Mitch sucked in his breath as she massaged him to full length.

It took him two tries to catch his breath, and when he did, all he wanted to say was, now!

He managed to bring his desires under control…barely, but he did.

"Stephanie—" He stopped as she turned around, dropped to her knees, and yanked the buttons open on his jeans.

Reaching in, she grasped his silky, hot penis and brought it out gently.

He closed his eyes as she brushed it over her gossamer lips and slowly swallowed his thick length, inch by rigid inch.

She hadn't meant to be greedy, but she couldn't wait to feel his length slide between her lips and wrap it with her moist, hungry, mouth.

He couldn't speak. Hell, he couldn't breath. Why worry about speech?

She swirled her tongue around the tip, down the side of it, then back up the top. She sucked directly on the head and managed to get her tongue in the hole to twitch it back and forth.

He was going to come right now and she had barely touched him.

She brought her hand up to cup his scrotum and used one finger to stroke his perineum.

He had never felt anything like it and opened his mind to share it with her.

Stephanie…feel—

Stephanie gasped around the penis she had taken deep in her mouth again and the sensations she felt caused her to suck harder. She felt every pull of her mouth on the silky rod she held, every swirl of her tongue. She had known she could hear and feel what they did, but his cock in her mouth felt as if it were attached to her nerves.

She opened her mind and Kristain immediately got up from the couch and left the baseball game he'd been watching.

She felt both Mitch's pleasure and Kristain's desire.

Kristain stepped out of clothing as he hurried to them.

Stephanie felt his mind reach out to grasp the sensation he was feeling from Mitch.

Even as she smoothed her finger back and forth across Mitch's perineum, she opened her eyes and found Kristain standing in the doorway, tugging the second pant leg off his foot.

She heard him thinking he wanted to bury his throbbing cock so deep inside her, she would still find him there in a week.

Shuddering, she closed her eyes and let the sensations enclose her in a world of their own.

Kristain had to stop in his progress toward Mitch and Stephanie. He felt as if Stephanie were gifting both him and Mitch at the same time. He knew if he wanted to join them he would have to bow out of the link for a short time.

He was loath to do it. He stood and let the sensations flow over him, then waited until they got too much, and he had to cut out.

He watched as Mitch came close to spending himself, then decided it was time to join in.

Kristain went behind Stephanie and knelt. Grasping her unresisting hips, he lifted her slowly and set her down on his lap. He wanted to thrust into her right away, but first was going to make sure she was ready.

He reached around her and grasped ahold of her left nipple as he used his other hand to delve between her nether lips and find her.

He gently rotated his finger on her bud in ever increasing circles. When she started to grind her hot core on his throbbing member, he reached further to make sure she was as wet as he could make her.

Finding her more than ready, he let go of her nipple and brought both hands up to her waist to lift her onto himself.

A tiny growl escaped from her full mouth and he hurried his motions. Placing his cock at her entrance, he opened both her and his mind. He didn't want to miss even one second of their joining.

Stephanie felt Kristain join them mentally, then suddenly, the mind link was gone. She hadn't wanted to miss even one second of what she was feeling and doing to Mitch, so she dismissed Kristain's leaving. No sooner had she done it than she felt him behind her. She wanted to beg him to come into and join them, but she was so into her feelings she couldn't think of much else.

She felt his hands around her waist and could have died very happily right here.

He made the sensations even better when he lifted her onto himself. Now, she waited as he paused with her over his pulsating cock and she waited for him to slam into her.

It wasn't long in coming and she convulsed the minute he rammed himself home.

In the corner of her mind, she felt Kristain's release, and soon on the heels of his, Mitch screamed in completion.

Stephanie swallowed as best she could while her release still pounded through her.

Chapter 14

The phone rang as Stephanie looked through the cupboard for something to make for dinner.

Since the men had come into her life, they had done everything for her. Tonight she wanted to cook something nice for them, and it looked as if she would have to go shopping again. Shaking her head at the amount of food Mitch and Kristain consumed, she picked up the phone and rummaged through a drawer for pen and paper.

"Hello?" She grabbed the items she had been looking for as her sister's voice came over the line.

"Steph? It's Jan." Although she could hear her sister, there was a lot of static, as if she was on a cell phone.

"Hey, Jan. I can barely hear you. Where are you?" Even as she sat at the table to make her list, she could picture her sister zooming toward some exotic locale.

"I'm headed for Catalina Island to do a catalogue shoot. Where—back? Homer has been in dire—when you'll be back?"

No matter how hard Stephanie tried, she couldn't understand what her sister was saying. Yelling over the static, she told her sister to call back when she could get a landline.

Not sure if Jan had heard her, Stephanie made a note to call Jan's agent and find out where her sister had gone. She'd get hold of her later.

When she finished with the shopping list, she went to find Mitch and Kristain to see if there was anything either of them wanted from the store.

Finding chocolate syrup and whipping cream at the top of Mitch's list, Stephanie rolled her eyes and jotted another note to pick up some extra stain remover.

Oh, she enjoyed what they did with the syrup and whipped cream, but getting the chocolate stains out of sheets could be a pain.

She'd managed to convince both Kristain and Mitch that she could handle the shopping by herself. Smiling, she thought of the looks both men had given her as they grudgingly agreed she was a 'big girl' who could handle herself.

Stephanie parked her Mazda in the supermarket lot and made her way inside. She grabbed a cart and quickly picked up the items on her list, stopping only in one extra section.

It didn't matter what store she entered, if it had a book section, she had to look. Some could call it an obsession, but Stephanie thought of it as very inexpensive therapy. Books to her were a kind of mini mind vacation. She thoroughly recommended it for everyone!

She ran her gaze down the available books to see if there were any new ones that hadn't been there last week. Finding none she didn't already have, she went to the checkout to pay for her purchases.

After she had emptied her cart, she scrounged through her purse looking for her cash and came upon the hastily made up wrap party invitation she had received from the last film she worked on.

A mental groan sounded in her head as she remembered she had already RSVP'd. She wouldn't be able to get out of this one. She had promised a few of the lighting and sound folks she would meet them there.

Hastily taking out the money she found, she counted out the bills and handed them to the cashier. Her mind raced to come up with any last minute excuse she could think of.

Think, Stephanie!

By the time she was halfway home, she still hadn't come up with anything not involving either a lengthy hospital stay, or some member of her distant family dead.

She pulled into her apartment's parking lot and parked her car. She finally gave up on finding an appropriate excuse and resigned herself to having fun. She wondered if Kristain and Mitch would like to go with her or if they would rather stay home tonight.

She grabbed her purse and prepared to get out of her car. She turned to reach for the door handle and found both Mitch and Kristain next to her car.

Holding back the scream locked in her throat, she hastily opened her door and got out.

"What? Is something wrong?" She quickly skimmed their thoughts and found they had come out to help her with the groceries.

Stephanie's smile could have toppled a government. It was what Kristain thought. Mitch concurred, and went a step further.

No, my brother, a Queendom. She will set the inhabitants of Aranak on their collective kujohs.

Kristain gave a tiny nod in agreement and gently took the keys from Stephanie's fingers. Both men went around to the trunk and quickly loaded their arms with grocery bags.

Stephanie had to stop and admire the complete maleness of the two men carrying her groceries. They took her breath away. Their bodies were everything a woman could ask for in a man. They both treated her as if she was their only concern, and they knew when not to intrude.

She vowed she would find a way to thank her sister in a very special way.

She took off to catch up with them and to ask if they might like to go out tonight. And after they got home, she would see if she couldn't find a special gift for them!

* * * * *

Stanley sat in his car and held the tiny device up as he strained to listen.

These gadgets always seemed to work in the movies and television, but when they were used in the real world, it was hit and miss. He only caught five or six words of what was said between the three, and they weren't any help at all.

He would have to sit here for the rest of the day and hope something else brought Stephanie out again.

The Slut, as he had come to call Babbet, had decided it was time to move.

He wanted to see just what else she really had in mind for Stephanie. Stanley thought a moment and decided he would only go so far for this woman, and as long as it didn't involve Stephanie Armand's death, he was open to most anything.

He took off the headphones and got comfortable. It could be a long night.

* * * * *

All three were putting away the groceries when Stephanie mentioned the party. The boys were enthusiastic and didn't mind at all. They teased her about wanting to show off her husbands.

Stephanie wondered just what they would wear. Both Kristain and Mitch had to have gone out at some point and brought back clothing to her —

She stopped the thought. She had been about to say her apartment when she realized it was now their apartment.

It took a second to sink in, but once it was there, it felt right. Yes, everything was theirs. At some point she would have to ask if the three of them might want to consider getting a house.

She put the thought away for now and went on with her speculation about clothing.

She had no more than started the thought when Kristain spoke into her mind.

We had a friend bring a few things while you slept Saturday. Stephanie heard him thinking. *Or maybe it was Sunday morning.*

Stephanie felt his mental shrug. *At any rate, we have proper dress. We won't embarrass you.*

Stephanie was shocked either one of the men sharing her life would think she was so shallow as to care about how they dressed.

Kristain. I can't believe you would think that! Stephanie didn't feel hurt so much as she was made to remember the three of them hardly knew each other.

With a thought she assured both Kristain and Mitch it wouldn't matter if they both wore diapers to the party, she had just wondered if they had any other clothes in the apartment or if they needed to go get some.

And after tonight, we're going to have to sit down and talk about more than me being Queen. We need to talk about where you guys come from, and how you use telepathy with great regularity. I know so little about the two of you, and I think we need to get to know each other a little better. Stephanie waited for a reply. None came, and she left it at that.

She hadn't meant to offend, or upset either of them, but she knew they needed to be face to face when the three of them talked this out.

Stephanie went to get ready. When she put her make-up on and did her hair, it was with the thought of wanting to look good *for* her men, rather than for herself.

When she was finally ready, she went out to the living room to find her purse and keys. She made another mental note to herself to get a few copies of her house and car keys made for Mitch and Kristain.

She was so lost in thought it took her a minute to realize Mitch and Kristain were already there and waiting.

She stopped in her tracks and gaped. They were absolutely gorgeous.

Both Mitch and Kristain had chosen to wear matching double-breasted suits. Their slacks were crisply creased and hit the tops of their spit-shined shoes just so. Their ties matched her midnight blue eyes, and blended well with the dress she had chosen to wear.

Either they were psychic, or they had "peeked". There had never been a worry in her mind they would have shamed her. Seeing them here together only confirmed this.

She continued to stare at the picture the two men made. She knew of more than a few people who would attend this party who would try their best to engage either or both of them in more than conversation.

When she thought more than a choked sound would come out of her mouth, she spoke.

"You look good enough to eat." Stephanie's eyes widened when she realized what she had said. She looked at the two men, who smiled with wicked intent, and continued on. "And as much as I'd love to indulge that statement, if we don't leave now, we're going to be more than fashionably late."

Stephanie picked up her purse and rummaged for her keys. She looked up when she heard a set jingle.

Mitch held up a set of keys as if to say "here they are."

"If you don't mind, we've taken care of the transportation." Mitch strode toward her and took her arm.

"Yes. Let us show you a little of what you can expect from now on." Kristain strode over and took hold of her other arm. "You did mention you wanted to know more about us, didn't you?"

Stephanie nodded. "Sure. You're more than welcome to drive tonight."

With that said, the three went out the door.

Chapter 15

Stephanie mingled with a silly grin on her face as she remembered the ride from her apartment to here.

Mitch and Kristain owned a truck. A really souped up kind of guy truck, and she had thoroughly enjoyed the smooth ride here. It shouldn't have surprised her they would own such a vehicle. They were, after all, men.

It was a truck with incredible power behind it and seemed to be comfortable to drive. Kind of like its owners.

Stephanie waved to a few acquaintances and had bumped into the director of the movie. She found out the film had apparently done well in selected theaters and been assured it would do even better when it went nationwide.

"STEPH!" The cry of her name at the man's highest decibels had Stephanie both cringing and smiling. Frank, the director of another of her shoots, was inebriated and thoroughly excited.

Turning to face Frank as both Kristain and Mitch's bodies whirled to face what they must perceive as a threat, she laid soothing hands on them both and smiled in genuine pleasure at the robust man coming toward her.

Easy guys. I think for the sake of my career, I'm going to have to disengage the mental connection for the party. Don't freak, okay.

Both men gave slight nods to her as she looked between them.

She cocked her head slightly as she heard Mitch answer.

If you perceive yourself in danger, it should automatically engage.

Sending mental thanks, Stephanie gave her complete attention back to Frank.

"Frank. I take it the masks did the trick?" Stephanie asked as Frank came directly up to her and enveloped her in a bone-jarring hug.

"You goddess, you! They worked! The masks worked! The moviegoers screamed in hilarity when the scene came up! Jesus on a crutch, they howled like friggin' banshees. It was exactly what the movie cried out for and shame on my cynical ass for ever doubting you!"

"Hey, you listened to my side of it. That in itself is a huge boost to my ego."

"Don't count yourself out. I'd had the thought and discarded it. You must have been in my subconscious and plucked it back out. I know others have said so, but you really can read minds, can't you!"

Even as the director laughed at what he thought was a joke, Stephanie looked to Mitch and Kristain and smiled. Frank was closer to the truth than he knew.

She felt pride in the job she had done and marveled at the truth others had liked her work. She knew it could have been a completely different story if the film had been a flop.

It was true. Sometimes in the film industry, all aspects revolved around the actual success of the picture rather than gaining merits for individual accomplishments.

They talked for a bit longer and both parted after promises to go to a theatre where Stephanie could watch the reaction of the crowd herself.

Stephanie thanked him for giving her the great news and moved on.

Stopping soon after, she turned to both Mitch and Kristain.

"Actually," Mitch interrupted her, "I have seen a few people we know."

"Great. There are a few people I want to talk to, so don't feel you have to stick next to me like glue. Besides, it'll be shoptalk. Probably bore you both to tears."

Kristain smoothed a hand down her arm while answering.

"Nothing you do or say would bore us. We live to hear your every breath."

Melting, Stephanie reached out and stroked her hand down the side of his face, then reached out to grasp the hand Mitch stretched toward her.

"You two will turn my head if you're not careful." Stephanie teased.

Bringing her hand to his lips and kissing it before he spoke, Mitch chimed in.

"I want to turn more than just your head *Kasha*."

My love. It hit straight to her romantic meter and knocked the needle off the charts.

"Go. Go say hello to your friends."

Smiling gently at the look of love in Stephanie's eyes, the two men left.

It was some time later that Stephanie realized she'd been socializing for longer then usual. So many of the crew had shown up believing that this was the film that would make their careers. Stephanie could agree that the crew was indeed right if the director had interpreted the audiences correctly.

She made a quick glance around the room for Kristain or Mitch and when she didn't spot them decided it was time to find some food to offset the champagne she had been consuming.

She wove her way through the tightly packed bodies near the refreshments and made a plate of goodies to nibble. She imagined either one of the men in her lives would have happily waited on her, but she had told them to mingle.

Stephanie smiled to herself when she noticed the olives on the table and then grinned foolishly at the memory of how Kristain had put them to use.

A feeling of near contentment spread over her and gave her a very encouraging picture of just what the future could be like with Mitch and Kristain.

She took her food to the nearest available empty surface and prepared to dig in. She had just started a fork full of chicken pasta salad to her mouth when she noticed someone standing in front of her.

"Hello Ms. Armand. It's a pleasure to see you again." He held out his hand as he spoke.

Stephanie automatically reached out and shook hands with him. It was a normal practice in Hollywood to interrupt someone in hope you could get a pitch in before you were dismissed.

The man looked vaguely familiar, but she couldn't quite place him, and she told him so.

He sat down as he explained to her he was a friend of one of the people who had worked on the film, and he had been admiring her work for some time.

He went on to explain he had visited the set a few times and seen her working. Not wanting to interrupt her, he had asked his friend to introduce him to Stephanie, but the opportunity had never presented itself.

He smiled sheepishly at this. "I must confess the only reason I attended this shindig tonight was to perhaps be able to meet you at last." He looked down at the table and then back up at her. "Please don't think me forward, but I couldn't wait for Renee to pull himself away from his date, so I came over to introduce myself."

Stephanie smiled with a mixture of relief and understanding. The relief came with the name Renee as someone she recognized. The understanding came with the sympathy she felt for this man. She herself had met Renee on the set of one of her first movies and found quickly enough he went through the men in his life like they were tissues. Use them a time or two, then discard.

It happened more often than not on a set, and everyone overlooked it as an alternate lifestyle.

"Forgive me," she started, "but you never told me your name."

At this, he looked startled. Then a slight flush came over his face. He smiled sheepishly and gave a small laugh.

"No. It's you who must forgive me." He grinned and introduced himself. "My name is Stanley."

Stephanie gave a quick thought to the food that still lay untouched in front of her and matched his smile.

"It's nice to meet you, Stanley. What do you do for a living?" Conversation in Hollywood was more than a staple of life, it was a sparring match that could get out of hand if not steered in a proper direction. Stephanie kept up a steady flow and managed to find out Stanley was an aspiring actor himself.

He had done a bit of stage, and come out to see if he could make it in what he called 'The Big Time'. Complete with air quotes and all.

They spoke for a good twenty minutes when Stanley finally looked at her plate and realized she had barely touched her food.

"Forgive me again. I do ramble." He gestured to her untouched meal and gave a look of contrition. "Your food is waiting there, and I've gone on long enough."

Stephanie waved it away and told him sincerely it had been her pleasure to sit and talk with him.

"Really, it wasn't a hardship. There's always more food, and it's rare to be able to sit and talk with someone as eloquent as you."

The look of pleasure, which came over his face at her words almost made her blush.

He watched her with a look Stephanie could only term as one of glee.

Stanley gave her a hurried farewell after that and told her he hoped to see her on another set soon. Stephanie waved to him and looked back down at her wilting pasta reluctantly taking a bite.

It was warm in the room, and the pasta outside of ice hadn't held up very well. She set her fork down and settled for nibbling on the few vegetables and fruit she had picked up.

When she was done, she turned her head to where the food lay and debated if she wanted to trudge back through the bodies that were still crammed into the small area.

She finally decided she would just stop and get something on the way home, and stood up to see if she could find either of her guys.

Stanley watched Stephanie leave the table, and waited. If she turned to the right, he would have to wait.

However, if she—

The grin crossing his face, if she could have seen it, would have sent Stephanie running in the opposite direction.

Stephanie opened her link to Mitch and Kristain and found them sitting with a woman she had never seen before. They each had frowns on their faces and appeared tense.

She felt Mitch return a thought to her assuring her both he and Kristain were fine. If she wanted to continue to mingle, go ahead. If she was ready, or wanted either of them, give a holler and they would find her.

Stephanie gave a delicate snort at the holler bit and wondered just how loud a voice could sound through telepathy.

Mitch gave her an image of him cringing, ears covered, and a look of pain crossed his face. Stephanie guessed a voice could sound in one's mind just as it could sound to one's ears.

Kristain joined them and gave Stephanie the equivalent of a mental stroke down her spine. She shivered and felt their love coming through.

She did her best to return the feeling and hoped they knew just how much she appreciated them not hovering.

She was so intent on the conversation she was having in her head she almost ran smack into someone.

Quickly looking up, intending to apologize, she found herself face-to-face with Stanley once more.

"Are you all right, Ms. Armand?" He braced her with his hands on her arms. She made a tiny sound of laughter and shook her head from side to side.

"Just fine Stanley. I was deeper in thought than I'd realized and wasn't paying attention to where I was going." She gave a rueful shrug. "I get that way sometimes."

She tried to concentrate on what he was saying after that, but Mitch and Kristain both interrupted her to ask if there was something wrong. They relaxed when she explained the mind speak could be a distraction. She was just learning how to do more than two things at once, that was all.

They sent her reassurances that she would get the hang of it soon, and she tuned them out.

She looked up once again at Stanley and he seemed more seriously focused on her than earlier.

"I'm sorry Stanley. I didn't hear what you said." She tried to give him a contrite look, but the look he gave her seemed to say she might not really be all right.

"Ms. Armand. I think you might need to sit down." He began to lead her toward the room that held the food and explained she probably just needed a breath of fresh air and some food in her.

He led her out the terrace doors to tables which had been set up outside. He helped her sit in a chair and told her he would be right back with something to eat. When she tried to protest, he rolled right over her.

"I feel badly." He began in an almost too serious voice. "I talked your ear off and you politely refrained from eating while

I did." When again she would have protested, he shook his head and held out his hand to stop her from speaking.

"My mother taught me better manners, and if I hadn't been so distracted with meeting you, I would have used them. Your mother did a better job teaching you manners."

Stephanie gave in and allowed him to go get her another plate. She told herself she would reassure him it was in no way his fault when he returned.

It was however the sweetest thing for him to do. She wondered if he might not have better manners than he was letting on.

She waited and found the night air did feel cool on her skin and she reminded herself to thank Stanley for the small treat.

He wasn't long, and she saw the heaping plate immediately. There was no way she could eat even half of what was on it, but she could share it with him. It was only fair, after all.

He set the plate in front of her on her right side. "There. That should help a little." She looked up and thanked him for his generosity. He grinned as if he had given her a great gift, then stood and waited for her to eat.

"Why don't you sit down and join me." She asked. "There's plenty here, and I can't possibly eat it all."

As she was turned back to tell him she didn't mind sharing, Stephanie watched as his hand descended onto her upper arm.

She felt a sharp pain and shot her head up to look into his eyes.

The pleased smile he had been wearing turned into an evil, wicked, leer.

She opened her mouth to protest, and tried to open her mind to scream for Mitch or Kristain. Nothing seemed to work. All she saw was a fast approaching darkness and a feeling of floating away from herself.

Darkness descended and she felt nothing more.

* * * * *

Mitch and Kristain stood abruptly. The link with their wife had been cut suddenly, and not of her will.

They sent out sweeping probes through the throngs of people who traveled from room to room, but felt nothing. No matter how much they increased the volume, their shouts went unanswered.

Mitch looked down at Babbet and abruptly nodded and excused himself and Mitch. For the past few minutes they had been telling her in no uncertain terms they were not interested in her or her pleading to continue their previous connection. The major point of this conversation was for her to leave Stephanie out of any of her future conversations. Upon their arrival at the party several acquaintances mentioned Babbet had been spreading gossip about Stephanie.

They'd said their piece; now, they didn't care. They just wanted to find Stephanie. They each gave an absent nod to the woman and went in a separate direction to find Stephanie.

Babbet watched in slight confusion as both Mitch and Kristain had suddenly stood up. They seemed to be hearing something she couldn't. She gazed around the room and found nothing out of the ordinary. But when she looked back at the two men, they hadn't moved. When she would have asked them if something was wrong, they turned to look at her, gave a quick nod, and left abruptly.

Babbet watched as they went in opposite directions and began searching the crowd.

When they had been together, it had seemed as if the two men were reading her mind. Now she wondered—

Getting up, she went to find that rat Labowsky. When he was nowhere around, she quickly went to find a quiet place to make a call. Before she could reach one, her cell phone rang.

"Hello?" Her voice could have charmed the birds from the trees.

"It's me." came the reply.

"Did you do it? Do you have the item I wanted?" Her voice held malicious excitement.

When the reply was an affirmative, Babbet's smile turned to malevolent glee. "Meet me at my house, and don't dawdle. If you've opened the package before I arrive, you won't like the consequences."

With the parting threat given, Babbet closed her phone and shoved it into her clutch purse. She hurried to find the party's host, offered her apologies for leaving early, and hurried toward her waiting limo. The driver hurried around to open the door even as she shooed him around to the driver's side.

"Just get me home, and I don't care how many laws you break. I have company who can't be kept waiting."

She climbed into the car and slammed the door behind her.

The car shot out of the driveway with a screech of tires and a plume of blue-black smoke.

Kristain and Mitch met almost where they had started.

Together they determined Stephanie was nowhere to be found. They had asked around and been told she had been seen with an elderly gentleman who had taken her out on the terrace. When they went to check, they had found only empty tables and chairs. No Stephanie, and no older gentleman.

"Do you think we could have missed her?" Mitch suggested. "She could have been here while we were there, and—" He shook his head as Kristain looked at him.

"Never mind. It was a hope. I know she's not here." He gave a frustrated snarl that made Kristain pat his arm in understanding.

Mitch went on. "I can't FEEL her."

Kristain agreed immediately. "I know. It's as if the link was cut but the essence is still there."

Both men looked at each other and didn't have the need of reading each other's mind in this matter. They knew if the link was cut for too long they would turn on each other, and one would kill the other.

They nodded grimly at each other and left the party, no thought given to offering their regards to their host.

Chapter 16

I'm in, were the first words she heard from the voice. The weak words were barely above a whisper, yet Babbet felt the pleasure and gratitude from the voice immediately.

The diminutive voice began speaking softly, instructing Babbet in exactly what it wanted her to accomplish. She would only need to stop two men from their goal and in the meantime, she would be provided with gifts geared toward her particular tastes. When Babbet was ready to start her project, she would be sent all she required.

Chuckling softly, the thin voice spoke into Babbet's mind, and Babbet listened closely.

The weak, yet melodic tones the conniving voice used soothed her as nothing else could. The voice always allowed her to get the most pleasure out of her games and to inflict the most pain. It would be the height of foolishness not to listen.

It had been so long since she had found anyone willing enough to appease her appetite for pain and blood she often wondered if she would ever come again. The voice assured her that if she cooperated she would never again have to worry about finding partners to give her the satisfaction she craved from her bed sport.

I will assuage every need you could dream of and some you would never have imagined. The frail voice promised riches in everything she did and Babbet would indeed claw her own eyes out for the things the voice promised.

Nodding her head in agreement with the voice, Babbet resolved to do anything and everything that was asked of her.

Babbet remembered the exact moment she became invincible. Her perverted sexual appetite had increased over the last fourteen months and gotten increasingly kinkier, not to mention more pleasant over the same period of time. Her taste for bloodletting had grown in direct proportion with the conversations within herself.

It all seemed so clear now! The glee which came with each slice, stab, or cut she inflicted during sex gave her the most delicious orgasms and had begun to thrill her more and more as the connection with the voice increased.

Babbet's sex life had flourished after the twins had left her and she reveled in her unique appetite for blood. Giggling to herself, she had the thought she could almost be called a vampire now! She didn't want to drink the stuff, but she so relished rolling in it, and using it for her aphrodisiacs.

It was extremely easy to manipulate the wants of the voice with her wants. The will of the voice however would not be denied and it was a pleasant coincidence both it and Babbet's wishes had meshed so well. Babbet would have paid for the privilege of beating the woman who had dared to take what was hers. This woman, Stephanie Armand, was going to see exactly what happened to anyone who crossed Babbet Carlson.

✽ ✽ ✽ ✽ ✽

The Crone's malicious smile played across Babbet's mouth as she listened to the thoughts flying through the human woman's head. The Crone cackled in glee as she remembered how she had slowly incorporated her own evil plans into its weakminded consciousness. It was truly a pleasure to now have a young body and malicious mind to work with once again.

"Poor, silly, misguided Sara. That stupid woman learned nothing from me if she thought killing me would get rid of The Crone. I told her, more than once, I cannot die! I should have known she only paid attention to what she wanted to hear and not to what I actually told her."

The Crone had indeed told her that the old body Sara saw her in wasn't her own. The only reason she'd kept it this long was the people of Aranak trusted this wizened woman, and it would take entirely too long to build up trust in a younger one.

The plans the Crone made fit easily into the frame of Queen Sara, and the vicariousness the Crone lived had been enough for the time. If she thought she wouldn't have as much fun as she knew she was going to, then perhaps she could go and thank that silly Queen Sara for the unintended progress of her plans.

This woman would do quite nicely.

The Crone couldn't believe she had not instigated the Queen's plan on her own behalf. It made things so much easier. Now all she had to do was finish breaking the simple mind already established in this body. When she did, she would be free to take it over completely and take back the throne that rightfully belonged to her.

Queen Sara and Stephanie be damned! She was the ruler, and she would show them all soon enough.

First things first. Let this puny mortal have her fun, the Crone would get her own satisfaction in the end. All she had ever needed was a new body.

* * * * *

The first thing Stephanie became aware of was a woman standing close to her. The next was physical discomfort. She tried to find words to express her situation but her tongue stuck to the roof of her mouth. She could feel her body, but her thoughts floated in and out of her mind. She did her best to focus her attention on the woman she had first seen, but the woman no longer stood in front of her.

"So. You're awake." The voice came from beside her and it took all her concentration to turn her head toward it.

There was the woman she had seen. She tried to wet her mouth, then tried to speak.

"Wha ah oo? Har a Iah?" Stephanie waited for a reply, or might have slept for a moment, but still, none was coming.

The discomfort in her wrist she felt made its presence known. She tried to ease the feeling by moving them but found they seemed to be stuck together.

Now who would have glued my wrist together? She thought to herself. But was then distracted by the woman's voice speaking again.

"Did you hear me? Are you awake?" The voice turned in direction. "How much did you give her? It was only supposed to knock her out for less than an hour."

Another voice joined the woman's and it was a man's, one Stephanie should have known.

"I gave her part of the amount you gave me. Since I didn't know how much alcohol she might have had...I only gave her...part of..."

Stanley trailed off as he watched Stephanie twist while tied to the freestanding chin-up bar Babbet had installed in her basement gym. Her movements weren't coordinated, but the picture she made intrigued him. He moved forward, almost as if in a trance, and came to stand beside Babbet.

Babbet watched as Stanley came to stand next to her. When he was close enough, she saw a glazed look had come into his eyes.

That look she recognized. She had witnessed the same glassy expression come over his face as she had commanded him to get down on his knees while she had circled him like a shark. She had held a whip and the sound of the crack it made every time she let it unfurl and snap made him shudder and shake and a wet spot form on his briefs.

She watched as he reached out with one hand to graze Stephanie's right breast with his finger and could have swallowed glass. No one, but no one, was going to look at another woman while in the same room with her and want the other woman more.

The red haze shading her vision caused her to stop thinking rationally. It was the only excuse she would admit to herself as to why she lost her cool.

She turned to Stanley and ordered him back. In her hand, she held a whip and tested her swing as she watched the woman who continued to writhe helplessly where she was shackled.

"Stanley." Stan heard The Slut's voice from far away. However, all his attention was focused on the woman who tried unsuccessfully to detach herself from the chin-up bar.

He knew if she hadn't been given the drugs she would have figured out a way to unhook herself. The only thing that held her arms up was a pair of leather cuffs locked together with snaps and buckles. Any person who wore them could easily unlock them. It was one of the reasons he had bought those specific cuffs.

Babbet had more interesting pairs, but these were perfect if they got caught, at anytime Stephanie could have let herself out of them.

Stanley looked up to see if it would happen anytime soon and realized until the drugs wore off, Stephanie was at their mercy.

He growled and forced himself to picture just what Babbet had in mind to do to the woman. What he saw had his eyes shutting and reaching down to adjust the bulge in his slacks. The images running through his mind now almost had him coming where he stood. He held on with everything he could and tried to picture something else.

When he finally felt under control, he opened his eyes and turned to look at Babbet.

"What? No balls?" She reached out to cup him and he hissed through his teeth. "No, that can't be it. I feel them hanging low and very full right here under this iron rocket," she moved her hand to cup his penis and he sucked in another breath, "which seems to be throbbing as if it will shoot straight out into space."

Babbet felt the wetness start to flow freely in her panties and sucked in a deep breath of her own. She knew eventually he would become so aroused she could lash out with the whip, and he would beg for more until she allowed him to come.

She was torn.

On the one hand she wanted to take her lust and anger out on the woman who had presumed to steal her men. On the other, she longed to feel the lash break over the rump of the man who had brought her so low she was willing, even at this moment to hand him the whip and let him have his way with her own body.

She knew he would wield the whip with great insatiability. She remembered the one time she had allowed him to try. He had brought her to a climax that came so close to those Mitch and Kristain had given her. Briefly it had her contemplating giving up her plan to drive Stephanie from the two men.

One thing had changed her mind. Stanley was just as wicked as herself, and she wanted the only competition in her life to be between Mitch and Kristain fighting over her attentions.

Stanley was looking at Babbet as if he wanted her to start on him rather than Stephanie. She hurriedly brought her thoughts back to the tableau before her.

Babbet stepped back, deciding to wait for Stephanie to awaken a bit more. She didn't want Stephanie to miss a moment of the pleasure she would find in her eyes when she woke, confused and shackled.

She composed her features into a semblance of hunger and spoke. "I want you to watch while I whip the woman. I want to see the pain on her face I inflict and have her know she is getting as much pain as she has given me. And above all, I want her to know someone else is witnessing her humiliation."

Babbet turned her head and brought her fist up to her nose. She had taken her hankie out of her pocket and was using it in as part of her melodramatic performance. She wanted Stanley to think she was overcome with emotion, and would have been shocked to know he already saw through her dramatics.

Stanley watched Babbet try to squeeze out a few tears and when none were forthcoming, buried her head in her hands.

He gave a snort of laughter. When she shook with her fake crying fit he thought about getting up to go stroke her hair in some semblance of comfort. But instead, told her he would do as she asked.

And he would. He also had a plan that entailed waiting. When Babbet was done, he would use Stephanie. He didn't want some doped up woman on drugs, he wanted one who would respond to him.

Not that The Slut needed to know it. No, he would watch Babbet give Stephanie a few swats, and then he was going to come and slake his lust with his Slut.

He watched Babbet raise her head, and found she had somehow actually managed to squeeze out a few tears. He reached out with his hand and gently swiped them away, and murmured a few trite words of comfort.

"Don't worry. I know you have plans for her, and we'll make plans for you. You won't be left in the cold." With that parting remark, he watched as a much happier Babbet walked over to where Stephanie hung and began to cheerfully rid her of her dress with key tugs and rips.

The stupor Stephanie had been in was beginning to recede. If she stayed still long enough her vision cleared even more and she began to get a better feel of her surroundings. She seemed to be in a room with the man who had introduced himself to her at the party and a woman who she still couldn't seem to place.

She wanted to shake her head and rid herself of the drugged feeling, and she had tried.

It had been a mistake. All it had done was make her more dizzy and nauseous. It had taken every ounce of will power she still had not to vomit.

It had felt like days had passed when Stephanie realized she was more under the influence of the drug than she had thought.

She heard voices continue to talk and wondered just what they had in mind for her. She didn't have to wonder long when she heard the woman announce he was to watch.

Stephanie had lifted her head enough to see the man Stanley and the woman who now held some kind of whip. She would have shuddered at its presence but knew if she started she would continue to shake until she fell apart.

She waited while the man had comforted the woman and then watched when she turned around and came toward her. She closed her eyes and tried the restraints at her wrist once more.

Stanly watched as Stephanie began to struggle once more.

When she stopped and looked up at the woman, Babbet gave her a gentle smile. "Please, continue to struggle." She reached out to Stephanie and took hold of the front of her dress. "It excites me."

Babbet gave a brutal yank and the front of the dress came away in her hands.

Stephanie held a scream in her throat and squeezed her eyes shut. She felt her dress slide down her body and did her best to concentrate on nothing.

The woman had said Stephanie's struggles excited her and Stephanie didn't want that. She controlled herself to the best of her abilities and tried to think of something pleasant.

As soon as she had the thought, a picture of Mitch and Kristain leapt into her mind. She pictured the three of them together the last time she had seen them and found it—

Pain snaked across her back and buttocks as she jerked forward. The scream of fright she had held in turned into a scream of pain she had no choice but to let go.

When at last the level of pain had receded to a dull ache, she took a deep breath and hung in her restraints panting.

When Stephanie was given a moment, a very brief moment, she found the only good thing to come out of it was the pain had cleared her mind.

If the woman continued to swing the strap across her back, buttocks, and shoulders, and Stephanie didn't pass out, the drug would very soon be out of her body completely.

"Ah, yes." The woman reached out to caress the red welts she had left on Stephanie's backside. There was slight warmth where she had laid the whip across her back. Warmth Babbet knew would grow into a searing fire for Stephanie and keep her skin hot to the touch.

The throbbing had subsided in her own cunt, yet it became an aching heat itself as she thought of what was to come. Babbet stepped back and continued her conversation with Stephanie as she raised the cat-o'-nine for another swing.

"I think a few more of these will do nicely. What do you say we give it a whirl?"

Babbet was doing a fine imitation of a dog in heat. She squirmed where she stood as she watched the lash coming down on the backside of Stephanie. It excited her to see this woman suffer.

She had attempted to use her words as another lash on Stephanie's mind but found with each stroke she swung, it made her breath leave her body and she had trouble holding on to her thoughts.

If she continued this for much longer she was going to climax and ruin the whole plan of torturing Stephanie.

Stanley stopped just short of climax himself. He sat in his chair and held perfectly still as he steadied his breathing. He continued to watch the woman who hung in cuffs before him and made little whimpering sounds.

Maybe he had gone just a little too far when he had agreed to kidnap her, but to see her wiggle and jiggle in nothing but garters, a demi-bra, and heels, had been worth every minute! It had driven him to whip out his cock and make use of the fantasy unfolding in front of him.

He turned his head and found Babbet with her hand down her skirt and Stanley smiled wickedly. He hadn't been the only one to enjoy the show.

Stanley turned back to Stephanie and made a decision. Getting up, he stuffed himself none too gently back into his pants, then took the syringe he had used on her earlier out of his pocket, uncapped it, and swiped at the sweat that ran down Stephanie's shoulder so her skin was unmarred.

When she gave a soft whimper, he hushed her.

"Easy. This will make it feel all better." He sank the needle into her arm and hit the plunger. It would soon take effect and then he would see if Babbet was as hot as her hand was making her at the moment.

He would need to hurry though. Somewhere along the way, the tube of the needle had leaked and there was very little of the drug left.

Stephanie waited for the relief to come and it didn't take long. Her last thoughts were where the hell are Mitch and Kristain!

* * * * *

Mitch and Kristain had gotten a description of the man seen leaving with Stephanie and were on their way to the apartment.

Neither wanted to think Stephanie had decided to take him home, or *Riad* forbid she had gone to his place.

But Mitch had known it could be a possibility. Both he and Kristain had decided they needed to check the apartment. They were on their way up the stairs when the first image flashed in their head.

Stephanie tied to a pole and a man, one who fit the description given of the man last seen with her, stood beside her with—

The image vanished.

The men stopped climbing the stairs and stood as still as statues. They sent out probes and screams alike to Stephanie, but to no avail.

It was Mitch who shook Kristain out of his attempts.

"Stop. It is gone." Mitch tried to sound practical. "We will continue—" It was as far as he got.

With a roar to do any lion like *avartar* proud, Kristain launched himself at his brother.

Mitch moved with the speed of their kind and managed to get behind his brother where he held onto him.

"Stop! It does not help our wife! Get control of yourself!" He repeated it, and variations of it, over and over for what felt like eternity.

When Kristain finally panted in his hold, he repeated it again and asked for a reply from his beloved twin. He could only pray they weren't doomed to spend the rest of their time together as enemies who would eventually kill each other.

Kristain sent an image of a still lake to his brother and tried to apologize.

"I'll let you go when you speak to me in a calm manner and don't try to end my life." Kristain knew it hurt Mitch to do this, and found he could push the feelings of helplessness back again.

He had in no way wanted to hurt his brother, but the fact there hadn't been direct contact with his wife in so long—

And then to have the image of her restrained and naked with another man—

He pushed those thoughts out of his mind also and spoke.

"Brother of my Blood, Brother of my Heart, and Husband of our Wife, it is I who should beg your forgiveness. I know not what—"

Mitch gave a strained shout and let his brother go.

He turned Kristain around and grasped him in a quick bear hug and then let him go by pounding him on the back.

"Brother mine. There is no need for a formal apology." Mitch starred at Kristain and continued to pat his brother on the back.

The strain both had been feeling eased a bit, and they both breathed a tiny sigh of relief that at least Stephanie was alive. It was something they had both felt, but seeing her had given them the measure of assurance they had needed.

Kristain returned the patting with a slug to his brother's arm. "Thank you, brother mine. I needed that."

They both continued up the stairs and went down the hallway to Stephanie's apartment.

Once there, they realized neither of them had keys.

"Well, it's not as if we can't get it fixed later." Kristain barely finished his comment when both raised a leg and slammed the door open. They didn't wait for it to stop and hit the wall as they just rushed in. The door never came near the two who went through the apartment with the speed born into them, gifted from their ancestors.

They met at the front door and found, as expected Stephanie wasn't in the apartment.

"As much as it pains me," Kristain started toward the couch with Mitch following, "we're going to have to go back over the flash scene we got. There may be—" Kristain trailed off and Mitch finished his thought for him.

"Yes. There just may be a clue in it." And maybe, they would be able to find their wife quicker.

Chapter 17

Stanley watched as Babbet knelt on all fours on the bed.

So far, he had only teased her.

She had come once, and he was prepared to go at it all night. Except the whip continually reminded him that another woman waited for his attention.

He watched as Babbet rocked back and forth and repeatedly thrust her bottom out toward the lash he wielded.

He made up his mind this would be the end to her fun for the night. After she had climaxed for a second time, he would leave her limp and sated and then see to Stephanie.

By then, she would be awake and willing or not, his.

* * * * *

Stephanie awoke to the feeling of pain. It wasn't nearly as bad as what she had felt earlier. She also felt a little more clearheaded than before.

She still felt fuzzy, but she knew where she was. She lifted her head and waited for the room to come into focus.

By the time it did, she was already struggling to get free.

It had taken her more time than she wanted to think about to get herself out of the laughingly easy cuffs Stanley and the woman had used.

Her mind had begun to clear even more when Stephanie stood up and had to suck in her breath at the pain in her back. Her arms were stiff and she had to stifle a scream. Her throat hurt as well, but she didn't want to alert anyone to the fact she was awake and free.

She waited until she could control the movements of her body and slowly shuffled toward the door.

She leaned into the door, putting her ear against it. She wanted to say she was listening for anyone, but she knew it was because she needed to rest for a moment.

When Stephanie felt she could move once more, she pushed herself off the door and gripped the knob opening it.

Her back burned, her arms hurt, her butt was still mostly on fire, and her feet felt like lead weights at the ends of her legs. None of it mattered, she was leaving, and nothing was going to stop her. The further Stephanie went, the more she started to feel the effects of the drug. She found if she stopped for anything, the feeling receded.

She tried to open her mind to Mitch and Kristain but couldn't hang on to the connection for any length of time.

So she focused on climbing the stairs she found and ultimately her way out of wherever Stanley had brought her.

Mitch and Kristain had gone over the scene that had flashed so briefly into their minds. They found if they didn't concentrate directly on Stephanie they caught glimpses of what was around her.

The one they continued to strain their inner eyes on was the image of a woman's leg and shoe in the corner of Stephanie's vision. But no matter how each tried to strain their vision, they couldn't make out who the woman was.

They decided to try one more time when they were given a barge of visions coming in fits and starts.

First there were images of stairs. No sooner had one flashed into their minds than it left quickly to be replaced by the image of a door at the top of the stairs. The next one to come through was an image of a chin-up bar, then restraints attached to it, then the door again.

Mitch and Kristain barely had enough time to send out a quick shout before the visions vanished and they could only pray Stephanie heard their calls.

Stephanie's head came up with a jerk as she thought she heard Mitch and Kristain calling to her. The sudden motion made her bend over and vomit.

When her stomach calmed and her head stopped spinning, Stephanie opened her eyes. Thanking and cursing the fates at the same time that she hadn't eaten very much at the party, she straightened up and turned back to the door she had been trying to open.

Her mind cleared enough for her to open the door, walk through, and look around.

She found herself in a short hallway. All she had to do would be to take a few steps and she'd find herself walking toward a door that should surely lead to the outside.

At least she hoped that was what happened.

Stephanie stumbled forward and used the wall to keep herself propped up. She reached the corner where the hallway turned into an even longer hallway and breathed a sigh of relief.

There, at the end of the hall, was what had to be the front door to the house.

She gathered the strength she would need to propel herself to the end of the hall and out the door.

When she was sure there was no one around, she started walking down the hall as quietly as she could. She strained her ears to hear any sound that might give her away, and also listened for any sound someone was around.

She managed to get to the door and was just beginning to open it when she heard a noise.

Stephanie listened for a moment and thought she heard grunting. She shook her head slightly and found her head was almost completely clear of the drugs.

She tried again to connect Mitch and Kristain, and focused on her surroundings.

She was focusing so intently she had to wonder if the shouts of her name were in her head, or coming from someone next to her.

Finally she gave up on sending images to her husbands when her head started to throb uncontrollably. She used what concentration she had left to open the door and slip out.

She was closing it when she heard the distinctive yell of completion.

Stephanie was sure the scream had come from the woman who had been in the room with Stanley, and the scream had held a sound of pain in it.

Shuddering, she quickly closed the door, and did her best to hurry down the steps to reach the sidewalk.

Mitch and Kristain both held their heads in unison as the vision slammed into them with the force of a brick.

When the pain had subsided enough for both men to see again, they found themselves on the floor. Mitch looked at Kristain and found he was as slow to get up as Mitch.

Kristain looked at his brother and wondered if Mitch had seen anything. He would have just looked into his mind if his own head hadn't pulsed as if someone had set off a bomb in it.

"Please tell me you saw whatever it was that laid us out." Kristain whispered it, but it still managed to make him feel ill.

Mitch looked as pale as Kristain thought he probably did, but managed to croak a response. "It was Stephanie." Mitch paused to take a shallow breath and prayed he wouldn't lose the food he had eaten at the party.

"She's in pain, and she is at Babbet's house." He swallowed once more and knew he was going to lose the battle with his stomach. He tried to stand and knew he would never make it to the bathroom.

It might have been a mildly cool night, but Stephanie shivered as if she was out in below freezing temperatures.

Part of it was from shock. But mostly, it had to do with the fact she hadn't bothered to find any covering before she left the house. She hadn't wanted to stop long enough to be discovered. She had also wanted to get out of there more than she had wanted her body covered.

She had used the grass to make her way off the property and onto the road so her feet would get less torn up. She followed the road in hopes she might just find her way to a phone.

So far, all she found were the rocks under her feet and the fact there wasn't a phone to be had in the whole neighborhood.

She kept her head down to avoid any further surprises under feet, and barely looked up when she heard a car.

The only thing she cared about was that it wasn't Stanley and that woman. There were probably other things she should have been worried about, but not running into Stanley and the woman was tops on her wish list at this moment.

The vehicle crossed to her side of the road and slowed to a stop. Stephanie continued to walk just in case it was Stanley and only stopped when she heard a familiar voice calling her name.

She gave a cry of relief and sank to her knees, heedless of the rocks and dirt stabbing into her skin.

She had managed to get away on her own, and help had finally arrived.

Kristain drove while Mitch scanned the area leading up to Babbet's house. He continued to get flashes from Stephanie and wondered why she couldn't hear them. When they found her, he would have to ask.

They were almost to Babbet's estate when they saw the woman walking along the side of the road. The headlights of the truck swept over her and what the two brothers saw made them flinch.

The woman was dressed in undergarments and nothing else.

And the woman was their wife.

Kristain brought the truck to a halt and both he and Mitch threw themselves out and toward their wife. Even before they reached her they saw the welts on her back and briefly each reached for the other. Then both moved at the same time.

They were on their knees and gently taking her in their embrace and holding her lightly. They did their best not to jar her while they both stood.

"Stephanie," was all either could manage.

Kristain looked into Mitch's mind and found both he and his brother were having the same thought. He shook his head in denial and began to pray. In fact, they both prayed. They prayed their wife had been able to fend off another man.

Again.

They reached their apartment, brought her upstairs, and debated taking her to the hospital. When she protested weakly, they compromised. They had a doctor friend come over and check her.

When the woman had arrived, she had told them to go away. They had told her no and continued to hang onto Stephanie, each of them taking a separate hand and holding on.

While the doctor had gone through her examination, both brothers crawled into their wife's mind and made a search of their own.

What they found enraged them even while they both breathed a sigh of relief.

They had seen things from Stephanie's view and found whoever the man was, he had definitely been excited, and he would have eventually done things to her which would have hurt her even more than the whip.

Mitch and Kristain found they both shook uncontrollably.

They will pay for their transgressions. Mitch made this statement in a strangled voice to Kristain alone.

Either with their lives, or with their minds, Kristain spoke in agreement.

As soon as the doctor announced Stephanie's back would heal, and she would probably need time to come to terms with the rest, Mitch and Kristain thanked her and told her if she ever needed either of them, not to hesitate to call.

After escorting her out, Mitch and Kristain again entered Stephanie's mind.

You will rest. The command came from both her husbands.

If she weren't so exhausted, Stephanie would have argued with the abrupt command. However, the way she felt, she had no trouble complying.

When they were satisfied she would sleep for some time, Kristain and Mitch went into the living room to plan.

They were going hunting, and no amount of pleading on the prey's part would sway them. The two were going to die!

* * * * *

"What do you mean she's gone? Didn't you restrain her?" Babbet screeched the questions at such a high decibel Stan covered his ears to drown her out.

Perhaps he and Babbet had indulged in a little more playtime than he had thought. And was it his fault both he and Babbet had fallen into a sound sleep once he had gained his satisfaction?

He gave a snort of disbelief. The shrew, screeching like a banshee, was going to drive him to do something she wasn't going to enjoy at all!

Chapter 18

Mitch opened the front door at the same time he opened his mind. When he found Stephanie still slept, he headed straight for the bathroom and the shower.

Kristain's mind had opened with his brother's and when he too found their wife still slept, he headed for the kitchen with the bag he carried.

Setting the bag down on the counter, he reached into a cabinet for two glasses. Taking them down, he turned around, and grabbing the bag off the table headed for the same bathroom Mitch had gone to.

Kristain poked his head into the bedroom where Stephanie slept to reassure himself she was really there and upon seeing her gave thanks again to *Riad* they had found her.

Turning, he left her and continued on to the bathroom.

Not bothering to knock, he opened the door and found Mitch had already stripped and was under the water. Kristain set the glasses on the counter then reached into the bag and took out the whiskey they had bought on the way home from their hunt. He broke the seal on the large bottle and poured a good portion of the liquid into both glasses.

He lifted one glass and stuck it into the shower where Mitch grabbed it from him. He picked up the second glass and drank it, not stopping until it was gone.

Shuddering as he felt the liquid move through him, he waited for Mitch to hand the glass back out to him. Instead, Mitch stepped out of the shower and took Kristain's glass from him.

Mitch grabbed up the bottle off the counter, a towel from the rack, and left with a mumbled "your turn" to Kristain.

Kristain began to strip out of his own clothing and was glad Mitch had left the water running for him. The hunt had been successful. But right now, they had both needed to wash it away from themselves and be with their wife.

He didn't take long in the shower either, but when he stepped out, he found his and Mitch's clothing gone. He sent out a question and found his brother had thrown them in the trash. Shrugging, he grabbed the other towel off the rack and began to dry himself.

He walked into their bedroom and found Mitch was just sliding between the sheets. Kristain watched as Mitch wrapped himself around their wife and held on as if she would disappear.

Kristain felt the same way Mitch did. He wanted to crawl into their bed and keep their wife in it forever. This way they would always know where she was. And they would always know she was safe.

Throwing the towel aside, he walked around to the other side of the bed and crawled under the covers so Stephanie was surrounded by both of her husbands.

Both men shook at the thought of what could have happened to her and this caused them to hang onto her tighter. They made a vow she would never be out of their sight again.

Stephanie was hot. And the bed was shaking.

Mumbling sleepily, she asked to have the heat turned down and then asked if they were having an earthquake.

It was also when she noticed she was being squeezed by a boa constrictor.

Or so her sleepy mind thought. It was the last thought, that a snake held her which finally brought her fully awake. She stopped struggling when she realized it was her husbands.

As soon as she relaxed, so did they. But the shaking continued.

She opened her eyes and mind and found they had been waiting for her to let them in. She wrapped them both in her conscious being and poured her love into them. It was only at that moment they stopped shaking.

She wiggled a little more and managed to free her hands. She used them both to touch each of her husbands and reassure them.

Mitch? Kristain? She thought and sent them both images of what she wanted.

Both men obliged her immediately.

Using exquisite care, both men managed to position Stephanie to where she was the least uncomfortable. She tried to tell them the only discomfort she felt was the throbbing ache between her legs.

When they ignored her insistence, she showed them instead.

She lay on her side facing Kristain. Reaching out her hand to his already burgeoning penis, wrapping her hand around it as far as she could, she began stroking it up and down slowly.

When she felt it was sufficiently lengthened for what she had in mind, she scooted closer to him and lifted her leg around his hip. She thrust her hip toward him as she used the same hand in which she held him to guide his ever increasing length into her drenched vagina.

She wiggled her hips until she was where she wanted, then laid still.

Mitch lay flush along the back of her body and she rejoiced in the feeling of his cock as it fit into the full breadth of the seam of her ass. They were both pulsing around and in her and she didn't want to wait a moment longer.

Sensing Stephanie was ready, Kristain moved slowly inside of her at first. But when she dug her nails into his shoulder, he picked up the pace. Giving his brother a gentle mind nudge had Mitch grabbing the tube of lube off the nightstand and Kristain felt Mitch coating his cock with the lube.

After, Kristain concentrated on Stephanie alone and began to ignite the flame of passion higher.

"That's it love, just like that." Mitch spoke into Stephanie's ear as she rocked her hips faster. He reached down and began reaming his finger around her puckered hole. Stephanie gave a tiny cry of surrender that sent his throbbing dick stretching another inch. It was all he could do to take his time and go slowly. She hadn't had much action back here, and he wanted everything she felt now to be associated with pleasure.

His mouth connected with her ear, and he began to bite and suck gently even as he began to coat himself again to enter her.

Sending a tiny thought to Kristain, he watched as his brother's head swooped down and captured their wife's mouth. Kristain ate at her mouth as if he would never get another taste again. Kristain's lower body ground into Stephanie's and Mitch began to enter her ass slowly.

The feel of just the head of his cock embedded in her made Mitch bite down hard on his own lip to stop from coming. She was tight, and hot, it was all he could do not to give into the urge to slam his full-length home.

Mitch gritted his teeth while he rocked his way into her tight ass and found he wouldn't last very long if the sounds his wife were making continued.

Stephanie stabbed her tongue into Kristain's mouth over and over again, waiting for the feeling of being full to bursting with cock to ease.

Feelings of both men inside her once again did a lot to ease her feelings of fear the abduction had brought up. Just being surrounded by her two strong, eager and able-bodied husbands made her want to cry out in joy.

But this feeling, it went beyond everything and anything she had ever felt.

She longed to move, but both men were using their cocks to pin her pussy and ass, and she wasn't going anywhere until they had made her come.

She whimpered in delightful agony as Mitch sank fully into her ass and Kristain worked his cock into her cunt. Both men came to a halt buried fully inside of her and the moan escaped her sounded like her orgasm was only seconds off.

"Please—" She didn't care if she begged. She would do anything right now for her husbands to move...just...a few...millimeters...so...she—

Mitch and Kristain both felt their wife riding the thin edge between pleasure and pain, and focused their attention on pushing her over the edge into pleasure.

Kristain pulled out slowly until he was half in and half out of paradise, then waited for his brother to do the same. As soon as Mitch began to pull out, Kristain began to stuff his cock back into her cunt.

They both continued the movements as their wife began to scream out her orgasm. Soon they both followed, they pumped their hips continuously into their wife until their own orgasms broke over them and shot their come deep into her body.

Mitch and Kristain labored long into the night in an effort to replace Stephanie's memories of the night before with ones of their own.

✳ ✳ ✳ ✳ ✳

The next morning did not start as well as they had anticipated.

"My Precious Jewel." Mitch and Kristain both said in unison. "It is with regret I—" as Mitch paused, he looked toward his brother and nodded his head, "or rather we, must confess—"

Mitch trailed off once again as Stephanie held up her hand.

"No. You're going to tell me—" Stephanie paused, then tried to continue. "That man and woman, I don't want—" She looked from one husband to the other, and sighed heavily.

"Some day soon you can tell me. But at this moment, I want it clear it was my right to—to take revenge!" She paused to make sure both men understood what she was saying. "I'm not some little delicate flower who always needs your protection. I could have found my way back and taken care of those two twits myself with no problem!"

Stephanie was confused as to how she was supposed to feel. Yes, there was gratitude her husbands had exacted revenge for her, but there was also anger that they hadn't waited for her to join them.

She also felt a tiny lingering of fear. After Rob, she had told herself she would never allow another to put her into that situation again.

Well, she had been, and she had gotten herself right out again. It made her feel empowered. As if she could manage any situation on her own as she always knew she could.

As petty as it might sound, it had been she who had been beaten, not they. She had wanted to see both Stanley and that woman again and exact a little of her own justice.

She shook her head at the thought of what she wanted to do to those two and wondered if what was done to her by the woman would leave her feeling frightened when she was by herself again.

She focused once again on the two men in front of her and gave another sigh. "Okay. I am grateful, yet more than a little confused at the anger I feel toward you two. I realize you had a right to—" Stephanie paused here and seemed to search for the right word she was looking for.

"…take action against, exact revenge, whatever you want to call it. I just wish you both would have allowed me the chance to…well, I don't know what I would have done, but at least I would have had the chance to do it."

Both men nodded to her in agreement, then decided their wife still needed more comfort.

"You may give us whatever punishment you think necessary for our infractions later." They both walked up to stand on either side of her and stroked their hands down her face and hair.

"Stephanie." They began in unison and spoke as if their minds were truly one, "Our wife, our Queen, the ruler of our hearts."

They paused for a moment and both looked deep into her eyes.

"We did what we thought was best. If you feel punishment for our actions is necessary, it is both your right and your privilege." They paused once again and Stephanie watched as both their eyes began to glow red. Anger seemed to infuse their face and the stance of their body became threatening.

"However, please understand it was our right, as well as our privilege and law of our realm, to seek out any and all who have brought pain to our house."

Stephanie felt the anger spilling from them, but in no way felt threatened. Their anger was not directed at her.

"Be they servant or family, no one will go unpunished when bringing worry, grief, or pain to those we love and cherish. The two sadists have been dealt with and will never molest another again."

They stopped talking and while the red receded from their eyes, the anger left their posture. They both shut their eyes and shook, ridding themselves of the rest of their negative emotions.

The intensity of their convictions was what finally made her decision. If she were truthful with herself, she would have done the same thing had someone managed to bring harm to either of her husbands.

They were right. There would never be repercussions for the retribution they had exacted on behalf of their wife.

She looked at both men and nodded just once.

"I agree it was your right. And the only thing I want made clear is if it happens again, I get to be in on whatever it takes to bring the culprits to justice. Is that clear enough for the two of you?"

Stephanie waited while her husbands seemed to confer with each other. She could have just opened her mind and eavesdropped, but she felt it would have been cheating. After all, this situation dealt with her as the wife really, not her as the Queen.

When the men turned back to her, they both nodded their heads and agreed in unison.

Chapter 19
Two weeks later

Stephanie allowed Mitch and Kristain to pamper her for a little over a week. Then she put her foot down and told them she was fine, and they really didn't need to continue waiting on her hand and foot.

Any want that popped into her head, one, or the other, and sometimes both, would jump to their feet and trip over the each other to get her whatever it was she wanted. It became comical, and she told them to stop. It had only taken them an extra two days to realize she really was feeling more like herself.

Her sister had finally called back, and both Mitch and Kristain insisted Stephanie tell her sister what happened. Stephanie had every intention of telling Jan, and had invited her sister to come over and have dinner with her and her new husbands.

The dinner had been a roaring success, and the night's lightness had gone a long way in helping Stephanie to deal with what had happened.

Jan had pulled her aside and as Stephanie had given her an abbreviated version of the kidnapping, commented on Rob once more.

"You know I'm here if you need me, I'll always be here if you need me. Just remember, neither Rob, Stanley, nor this Babbet woman has been able to break you. You are so much stronger than those maggots that you were able to avert any and all plans they had for you."

Jan had continually reminded Stephanie she was strong, good, and none of either episode could make her anything less than what she already was.

Stephanie knew Jan was right, and continuously reminded herself of it for the last week. She knew it would take time, and talking about it with her small family seemed to help more.

She pushed the thoughts aside for now and focused on the issue she had brought up to her husbands only moments before.

"I want to discuss us moving into a house. I always thought when I married, I would move into a house." She looked around the living room where she sat on the couch and wondered if either man had anything they wanted to move in, but didn't think there was enough room for it.

"Granted this is a two bedroom, two bath apartment, but I'd like something a little bigger."

She stopped glancing around the room and looked again at her husbands. "That reminds me. Are we going to be living off my salary, or do you two have incomes which can be transferred into this world's money?"

She could well believe she hadn't asked before. After all, she made a good living in her line of work. But it had wandered into her mind now and again since they had told her they were married, and she wanted to ask about it now in the interest of how much she would need for a house.

Kristain smiled gently at his wife and went to sit next to her, "I can't believe we haven't told you." He looked as Mitch sat on the floor in front of her and took her hand.

Kristain continued, "Our currency is the same as Earth. Mostly." He reached into the pocket of the pants he wore and drew something out.

He handed it too her and began speaking again. "This is also currency. Along with the bills and coins of this realm."

Stephanie looked down at the rock he handed her and sucked in an astonished breath.

She wasn't an expert on gems, but in her hand, she held what had to be a 15ct diamond. She watched as she turned the gem back and forth in her hand and the light from the window shone through it. She vaguely heard Kristain as he made sounds about how currency worked on Aranak.

"Um, I don't mean to interrupt, but does this mean we won't have to worry about money? And do you want me to start looking for a house?" Her question stopped Kristain's words as she looked back toward him, eyebrows raised.

Kristain took Stephanie's other hand in his and smiled softly at her.

'Tell you what. Why don't we sleep on it now, and in the morning we'll start our hunt for a house?" Even as he spoke, he brought her hand to his mouth turning her hand palm up and scraping his teeth and tongue along her palm.

Mitch smiled lovingly at Stephanie and watched while Kristain grabbed hold of Stephanie and brought her into his lap where he held her in his arms.

"Now that we're all in agreement about the house, let's talk about the babies we're going to give you which will eventually lead our nation," Mitch watched as her eyes began to take on a glazed look.

"OK. We'll talk about it in the morning too." He reached out toward her shirt and began to use his fingers to circle around her nipple. "For now, why don't we just get some practice in making them. What do you say, hmmm?"

The deep sexy tone of Mitch's voice ran through Stephanie heating her blood while it began to stir her juices. Kristain added his opinion in a way so she was feeling it instead of hearing it.

Smiling lovingly, Stephanie nodded her head and added her own thoughts.

"I'm sure the two of you won't have any problem practicing day after day after day, will you?" Reaching out with both hands, she wrapped her hand around two very impressive hard-ons, stroking them and feeling them enlarge.

"No, I don't think either of you will. Now, husbands, take me to bed so I can love you day and night, for the rest of our lives."

Both men smiled wickedly at her and said in unison, "Why not start right here?"

Her answer was swallowed between them as Mitch locked his lips against Stephanie and proceeded to leave her speechless. Not to be out done, Kristain took hold of her shirt, lifted it to bare her breast and latched his mouth onto one of her nipples. Lifting his head quickly, he grasped onto the extended nipple with his fingers and tweaked it.

Mitch lifted his head and traded places with his brother, latching onto Stephanie's distended nipple and sucking until he heard her moan with pleasure.

Kristain placed his mouth on Stephanie's and gave her his own promise with a kiss.

Through all three of their minds, one mantra ran.

I will love you even through death.

Epilogue

Shan Lin looked toward his brother Vincent. They both knew their "orders" came from the Queen herself in this situation, and the situation had gone from bad to worse over the last few weeks.

After Ranik, they had been sent to a remote camp on the outskirts of Aranak to settle some minor dispute happening on one of the Queen's holdings, only to find the villagers surrounding the camp in an uproar over the Queen's actions. Their grievances were valid. The Queen had been gathering their lands illegally over a long period of time and forcing out those villagers who wouldn't comply with her edicts to hand over their land.

Shan Lin and Vincent were left little choice but to follow the Queen's orders and imprison the rowdy few who had incited the violence. That taken care of, the villagers dispersed, angry still, but finding they had little choice.

If things continued in this vein, all the proof they had risked their lives to gather in an attempt to convince Mitch and Kristain of the position Queen Sara had put Aranak in would be for naught.

After reporting to the Queen things had quieted, Shan Lin and Vincent had gone back and asked if they could be allowed a bit of personal time. As pleased as Queen Sara had been with them, she'd allowed them both to do as they pleased for a bit. Her exact words had been crude and left the men sickened.

"Why don't you find your cousin Theresa, I'll lend you the housekeeper, and you can show both of them a good time while I watch. It'll be a study of youth verses experience I'll enjoy, and you'll get laid."

She had roared incessantly after her suggestion, and the idea had so appalled both men, they quickly took their leave.

Knowing the term "a bit" could mean anywhere from an hour to a month, both men had hurriedly made preparation for their journey to the realm of Earth.

"We haven't any choice, Shan Lin. We've got to tell Mitch and Kristain what was done to Dorian and pray Theresa never finds out."

Shan Lin nodded his head. He knew if Theresa, their cousin who also stood by their sides in the Queen's Guard as a high-ranking Captain, would use her considerable skills to see Queen Sara dead for what she had done to Dorian.

"I can't believe the boy thought he'd move up in the court if he slept with that vindictive bitch! What the hell did he think she was going to do, give him a title and send him on his merry way?" Vincent raged as he sent his fist swinging into a nearby tree trunk.

"You know what it's like to come into money and be recognized by the Queen. The only way we escaped notice was because it suited her to send us as far from her as she could get us. We earned our cynicism the hard way." Shan Lin spoke as he waited before the portal opening.

"Besides, the information Dorian had to impart was priceless. It's true it isn't quite the way I'd have gone about finding out what was going on in the Queen's mind, but you have to admit it's helped us put the final pieces together."

Vincent's grunting answer made Shan Lin smile.

"We're going to take down the Queen and we have to do it before she destroys our home. We have to find the Princes and this is the only way it can be done secretly. Our cover story of going to find a bride is perfect. So much the better if we actually bring a woman home with us."

"Find a bride. Mustn't forget to find a bride I don't want," Vincent snorted. "Look, I know we're going to have to follow our Princes and tell them their mother is the scourge of our realm, but I don't have to like it. I still think we could find a Tractow sorceress to impart the message to Mitch and Kristain." Vincent grumbled as the brothers prepared to open the portal to Earth. "You know I hate it when this damn thing lands us so far from our intended destination! The last time it took us *four* days to cross a damn mountain only to find out later we could have gone *through it* in hours instead!"

Shan Lin laid a consoling hand on his brother's shoulder. "It's all in the way you look at it, brother mine. The last time we were dropped in the middle of an unfamiliar area, and we spent the night catering to one of the horniest women I have ever had the pleasure to meet in my life! The walk through the desert was worth damn near every scratch and bite she left on my body." With a smile of reminiscence, Shan Lin gave his brother a friendly pat on the back stepping toward the ever-widening misty portal. "Besides, we need to find out if it's true."

"If what's true?" Vincent asked.

"Queen Sara's throne will soon be usurped and the new Queen is truly willing to relocate to Aranak."

With a malicious grin riding his mouth, Vincent walked into the chasm, a gleeful note in his voice, "One can only hope and pray it's true, brother. Hope and pray."

Enjoy this excerpt from:
QUEENS' WARRIORS
© Copyright Mari Byrne 2004

All Rights Reserved, Ellora's Cave Publishing, Inc.

Shari had done it. Finally, she had freed herself from the bump and grind of nine to five. No more setting the alarm for o'dark thirty to primp and prepare herself for a day of closed in office space. No more conferences, meetings, lunches, or drop-in surprises for this lady. No sirree, Phil! She was free to pursue her dreams of…

Shari paused on her trek down the hall to Karen's apartment and grimaced in pain, both mentally and physically. Her body ached in all the wrong places and her mind vacillated between thoughts on what exactly she would do now and focusing on the minor accident she had just been in.

Sighing silently, she made her way down to Karen's door. All she wanted to do was get inside and crash on the nearest flat surface. Walking as fast as her sore body would allow, forcing one foot in front of the other, she made her way down the hall.

Lord, my head hurts.

The scrape down the side of her hip had left her body aching and throbbing, and she would be lucky if she lived long enough to reach the apartment's door.

Stop it. You're exaggerating because you're doing your best not to freak out about handing in your two-week notice.

Smiling wryly, Shari White pushed thoughts of worrying about not having enough money in her savings account, having to tuck her tail between her legs and go back to a "real" job, and now the pain her body was signaling to her. The tiny aches and pains from the accident were becoming more and more intolerable by the moment. Shari supposed walking home after the accident hadn't been the smartest thing she could have done.

Shari stopped in front of Karen's door.

Finally, she thought as she reached her friend's door, *I can go in and crash!* Fumbling her key out of the pocket of her ruined pants, she unlocked the door and stepped inside. Shari dropped her purse and the equally ruined briefcase where she stood and turned to push the door closed, allowing it to shut behind her.

Immediately the doubts began to creep in once again. Would she be able to find something she truly enjoyed doing before her "Freedom" money ran out. Shari had given herself what should be a year's "cushion" of money to pay necessities, minor frivolities, and if needed emergency spending money.

But can I?

Her muscles interrupted her second thoughts, screaming viciously in protest as she walked forward. She was determined to land on a soft spot this time, and not settle for curling into a little ball of pain in front of the door.

"That's all I need. Karen would come in and smack me on the other side of my aching skull to make a complete job of it."

Even talking quietly out loud hurt her head too much, so she concentrated on making it to the couch and thinking thoughts softly.

The car coming out from the underground garage probably hadn't been going more than five m.p.h. The poor rattled driver had been coming up the blind ramp faster than he had thought and, *Bam!* Knocked her clean off her feet. But when the car had rammed into her, Shari felt as if it had been going at light speed.

She had been dazed, but other than probably needing an aspirin, she was pretty sure her injuries did not need a doctor. She flat refused to have an ambulance called. She hadn't lost consciousness, and most of the abrasions only needed bandages and cleaning. She would be fine once she got home.

"Not too smart, was it, Shari 'you're a twit' White?" Shari mumbled, wishing someone was there to whine to.

As pain continued to lance its way through her head, she remembered her comment not to talk out loud. Maybe if she just whispered. Besides, she did not have time to spend seven hours sitting in an emergency room somewhere in the city waiting to be told she was fine, go home. She knew her body well enough to know she would probably be fine in a few days.

Turning slowly, she spotted the couch and stumbled to it. She was on the verge of simply falling on it, carefully, and sleeping for a week, when a hammering noise sounded against the front door.

No! She gripped her head as the noise reverberated against the inside of her head. It would just top her *Day from Hell* if it ended up being a damn salesman intent on getting someone to buy the five thousand dollar set of encyclopedias, which would become obsolete the minute the next *coup d'état* in Peru erupted.

Wasn't there somebody trying to take over Peru at the moment?

Shari's head throbbed as her thoughts scrambled around in her head. Inconsequential things popped up and chased after one another until the pounding at the door started once again.

I could just ignore it, pretend there's no one here.

She grimaced at the thought. She had never been able to ignore answering a knock at the door or a ringing phone.

The pounding thundered again.

Muttering low in her throat and immediately wincing at the renewed pain, Shari forced her body toward the door. Standing slowly, she started to rise. It took her longer than she would have thought as her head began to whirl. Raising her arms with difficulty, she held her head between her hands long enough for it to stop doing merry-go-round imitations, then started for the door.

Shit! The heartfelt, whispered word ran through her.

Not bothering to check through the view hole in the door, she braced herself with a hand on the doorknob and wrenched the door open, leaning heavily against it for support.

Truly, she had every intention of stripping skin off whoever stood on the other side. Until, that is, she came face to face with the pair of sex gods. Her words died a flaming death. The pain, which had so recently radiated through her body, fled.

There stood two of the most gorgeous men she would ever lay eyes on. In front of her were two six foot five, muscle bound, sable haired, chiseled jawed, Chippendale dancers. Animal magnetism rolled off the pair in waves, making her pussy weep.

Taking shallow breaths, Shari saw black spots appear before her eyes.

"Please…"

She drew in the last of a shallow breath and let out a moan so close to a howl she almost scared herself. Her vision went gray at the pleasure streaking through her body and she fell to her knees, the pain in her body forgotten. Her head would have hit the floor as she bowled over if not for a skin-roughened hand slipping between her forehead and said floor.

Shari felt herself grind her hips on an erection she was sure was between her legs. She ground down as if riding a man, then gave a final shuddering scream as an orgasm rolled over and through her body in mind numbing bliss.

It took a few moments to gather her scattered thoughts. Panting in the aftermath, Shari felt muscled arms surround and cradle her body as if it was a delicate piece of porcelain. Turning her head slowly, she looked up into a pair of eyes the color of a sunset and had to blink, thinking she was imagining things.

The eyes she gazed into were glowing.

Squeezing her eyes closed in hopes she was seeing things, she blinked several times, then looked once again.

Nope. Not glowing at all.

She stared into two different colored eyes. One a golden bronze, the other the color of crisp, green, summer leaves. She closed her eyes once more and shook her head slightly for good measure, vaguely remembering her headache. When she opened her eyes again, she still saw the same set of eyes, both different colors.

A voice, low and resonating sensations against her stimulated body seemed to be making soothing sounds to her.

Tilting her head back a little more Shari took in the whole picture. She seemed to be in the arms of one of the men who had stood on the other side of Karen's door.

"Er…should I thank you and be offering a cigarette about now?"

About the author:

I have been writing for quite a while now and love finding out what goes on in the minds of my characters. I am the daughter of a third generation military family who grew up all over the world and happily married to a loving husband who gifted me with two adorable children I had the pleasure of birthing. All three enjoy dragging me away from my characters and showing me the world "outside". (I still think camping should involve "Room Service"!) I am also a voracious reader who devours books and chocolate in between family, writing, and work.

Mari welcomes mail from readers. You can write to her c/o Ellora's Cave Publishing at 1337 Commerce Drive, Suite 13, Stow OH 44224.

Also by Mari Byrne:

Queens' Warriors
Death Reborn

Why an electronic book?

We live in the Information Age—an exciting time in the history of human civilization in which technology rules supreme and continues to progress in leaps and bounds every minute of every hour of every day. For a multitude of reasons, more and more avid literary fans are opting to purchase e-books instead of paperbacks. The question to those not yet initiated to the world of electronic reading is simply: *why?*

1. *Price.* An electronic title at Ellora's Cave Publishing runs anywhere from 40-75% less than the cover price of the <u>exact same title</u> in paperback format. Why? Cold mathematics. It is less expensive to publish an e-book than it is to publish a paperback, so the savings are passed along to the consumer.

2. *Space.* Running out of room to house your paperback books? That is one worry you will never have with electronic novels. For a low one-time cost, you can purchase a handheld computer designed specifically for e-reading purposes. Many e-readers are larger than the average handheld, giving you plenty of screen room. Better yet, hundreds of titles can be stored within your new library—a single microchip. (Please note that Ellora's Cave does not endorse any specific brands. You can check our website at www.ellorascave.com for customer

recommendations we make available to new consumers.)

3. *Mobility.* Because your new library now consists of only a microchip, your entire cache of books can be taken with you wherever you go.

4. *Personal preferences are accounted for.* Are the words you are currently reading too small? Too large? Too...**ANNOYING**? Paperback books cannot be modified according to personal preferences, but e-books can.

5. *Innovation.* The way you read a book is not the only advancement the Information Age has gifted the literary community with. There is also the factor of what you can read. Ellora's Cave Publishing will be introducing a new line of interactive titles that are available in e-book format only.

6. *Instant gratification.* Is it the middle of the night and all the bookstores are closed? Are you tired of waiting days—sometimes weeks—for online and offline bookstores to ship the novels you bought? Ellora's Cave Publishing sells instantaneous downloads 24 hours a day, 7 days a week, 365 days a year. Our e-book delivery system is 100% automated, meaning your order is filled as soon as you pay for it.

Those are a few of the top reasons why electronic novels are displacing paperbacks for many an avid reader. As always, Ellora's Cave Publishing welcomes your questions and comments. We invite you to email us at service@ellorascave.com or write to us directly at: 1337 Commerce Drive, Suite 13, Stow OH 44224.

Printed in the United States
24338LVS00001B/175